KEEPING CLAIRE

KB ALAN

Copyright © 2010 by KB Alan

Edited by Jillian Bell
Cover Art by Fantasia Frog Designs

All rights reserved.

No part of this book may be reproduced in any form or by any electronic or mechanical means, including information storage and retrieval systems, without written permission from the author, except for the use of brief quotations in a book review.

First Edition: November 2010; Second Edition: January 2017

❀ Created with Vellum

For Jesse, who believes.

Big thanks to Viv for helping me get my butt in the chair and my hands on the keyboard, and to Jilly for making me think it all through.

ABOUT THIS BOOK

Keeping Claire

Claire's been fantasizing about the owner of her company since she first saw him. Ryan is gorgeous, confident and sexy as hell. In other words, so not her type. With the crazy life she leads, she needs to stick to men who are happy to do what she tells them to, then disappear. Since Ryan would never abide by those terms, it's best to keep him right where she's got him—in her dreams.

Ryan gets up close and personal with Claire while investigating a threat to his company. Once he's convinced she's not out to hurt what he's helped build, he refocuses his Fae energies on his intriguing employee. When she quits, insisting it's best if she leaves town, he's determined to convince her otherwise. At least long enough to get a taste of her. And the more he tastes, the more he touches, the more he wants. Now he just has to convince Claire that what they have is worth fighting for, and he's more than up to the task.

To join KB Alan's newsletter, visit www.kbalan.com/newsletter

CHAPTER ONE

Movement in the doorway to her office had Claire lifting her head. Her stomach clenched tight with the effort of not reacting to the sight of Ryan and Jacob standing in her doorway. There was no good reason for the two owners of the company to have come looking for her—a hard-working but mid-level paper-pusher. Clearly, the shit had hit the fan.

Ryan Diel took a step forward, his hard body stiff with anger. *Shit, shit, shit.* She'd kept to herself and worked hard for the company—her small way of making up for any trouble she might inadvertently cause them. Their complete collapse, for example. Which meant the only reason for his rigid stance was that they'd discovered something about her. And there was nothing good about that possibility.

She rose, slowly pushing her chair back with her legs. Ryan took another step forward when she opened the desk drawer, so she angled her body, allowing him to see the purse she pulled free. He held out his hand and she gave the bag up without question. Oh yeah, this was bad. Lips she'd fantasized about tightened as he studied her face. She made certain he saw only the blank expression she'd honed with years of practice. Which seemed to piss him off.

He narrowed his bright-green eyes for a minute before turning and walking out of the room.

She allowed a tiny hiss of breath to escape before squaring her shoulders and following him out the door. Focusing her attention on the taut ass in front of her helped tune out the sights and sounds of her coworkers as they watched her being led to the large office Ryan and Jacob shared. She needed to get out of the building fast, but it was suddenly occurring to her that the brilliant idea to work for a security company had been about the stupidest move she'd made in five years.

At her previous jobs, if human resources or management had called her into the office for an unexplained reason, she would have just left and been in a new city with a new name in a matter of hours. Only now did she realize that cardboard-box manufacturers and small bookstore owners were going to react differently than security specialists. Damn it, what had she been thinking? Clearly she hadn't been thinking enough. Maybe five years had worn her down more than she'd realized. She remembered hitting town and walking past this building three or four times before deciding that maybe she'd be safer at a company whose records couldn't be hacked. *Stupid, stupid, stupid.*

Understanding where she'd gone wrong wasn't going to help her now, though, and she was an idiot to be wasting time thinking about that rather than how she was going to get out of this building. Regret caused acid to churn in her stomach. Though she'd been careful not to make friends, Teck Security was a good company with friendly, helpful employees and caring owners. She should have left three weeks ago when she'd found herself joking with the receptionist as they walked out to the parking lot. Over the years, she'd rarely interacted with her coworkers, leaving them with the impression that she was a bitch. She probably was a bitch, but not the way they thought. It just made it easier for everyone when she had to leave without notice.

Ryan entered their office and she followed, Jacob close on her heels. That the blinds had already been pulled was about all she had time to notice before she was pressed up hard against the now-closed door. Her whole body went stiff, but she concentrated and relaxed her instinct to fight. Ryan searched her expertly, but under the circumstances, she was shocked to feel a tingle in her breasts as he passed over them. There was nothing inappropriate about the way his hand brushed between her legs, but her stomach clenched, and it wasn't in fear.

The heat of his body left her in a rush as he stepped back. She had to lock her knees to keep from trembling, though from adrenaline or fear she wasn't sure. Jacob gestured to the couch and she forced herself to walk to it slowly and sit as if she'd been invited to a meeting, not thrown against the door and searched like a criminal. If there was one thing she knew how to do and do well, it was pretend that a crazy situation was perfectly normal.

Vaguely aware that they were going through her purse and examining each item, she scanned the room for a way out. The huge furry face of Jacob's dog, Took, watched her from the side of the desk. As if the two large men weren't enough to keep her from making a dash for freedom, how could she forget about the enormous mastiff, Jacob's faithful companion? Every time she'd seen him before she'd had to resist the urge to get down and hug him. Funny how that was the farthest thing from her mind right now.

She returned her attention to the men since she was clearly stuck in the room until she managed to convince them to let her out. Jacob was examining her antacid packet, the pain reliever bottle already discarded next to the lotion and the lip balm. Her own damn mini pharmacy. It took her a puzzled moment to figure out that they were searching for some sort of electronic device. That was a good sign. They'd figured out that she wasn't who she'd claimed to be, but didn't actually know who she was or why she was there. They probably thought she was a corporate spy or embezzler or something along those lines.

More than five minutes had passed and they'd yet to say a word, but that didn't bother her. She had plenty of experience sitting still and remaining silent. If they thought to unnerve her, they were in for a surprise. Finding nothing in her purse, Jacob returned the items to it while Ryan opened her wallet. He didn't seem surprised to find all identification in the name they knew her under. She used the time to resurrect one of her favorite fantasies, one that involved running her hands through his curly brown hair while his mouth did delicious things to her breasts.

The thud of her wallet being dropped on her purse had her blinking back into reality. Finished examining her belongings, which she would be dropping into a trash bin first chance she got, Ryan and Jacob walked over to stand in front of her. Though Jacob was slightly taller than Ryan, they were both over six feet and towered above her as she sat. She didn't even attempt to make eye contact—if they wanted her to look them in the face they were going to have to come down to her level. In the meantime, she was staring right at Ryan's zipper and wished he were wearing jeans instead of slacks. A small twitch of the fabric invited her to lick her lips, but she resisted. Just barely.

Chairs appeared and the men sat. She still wasn't at eye level but she didn't want to push things and sat back against the couch so that she could see them better. Her leg automatically came up to cross over her knee and she was startled to feel her cheeks flush when Ryan's gaze followed the motion and remained riveted to the hem of her skirt.

Fuck. This was not good, she shouldn't be reacting to him. No lust, no embarrassment, no anger, no fear. No shame for bringing trouble to their company. Reactions were deadly. She lowered her foot to the ground and hardened her face once again. Ryan blinked and Jacob looked curious. That was fine. It was a lot better than most other reactions they could be having. They could hate her or forgive her, as long as she got away and never saw them again. If she could get away before those looking for her caught up to her, they might not lose their business. Or their lives.

"Miss Fiordalisi—" Jacob began.

"Please," she interrupted, "call me Claire."

She'd picked the last name because it had seemed amusing at the time to watch people try to say it, but it wasn't funny now. How could she forget, even for a second, that the people she encountered every day were in danger because of her? Now the idea of laughing at their expense made her sick.

"Claire. It would be best if you explained yourself."

He didn't say anything more, didn't say "or else" out loud, but she knew it was there. These men were trained in security, what the hell had she been thinking? This was nothing like the time she'd had to run out on the one-hour photo lab owner in the middle of a roll of thirty-six, his mouth hanging open as she called out over her shoulder that she wouldn't be back. These guys wouldn't just stand and stare as she moved on.

"Right. Well," she said.

Damn, she had no idea what the best way to handle this was. When she'd first started running, she hadn't given much thought to what kind of explanations she might give. And she rarely needed to. The few times she'd been in such a situation, where she had to talk before she could run, she'd just told the truth. Most people were happy to see the backside of her then. But these guys were different. And, again, that was her own stupid fault.

It occurred to her now, far too late, that if they believed her, they were going to want to help. Which would lead to them getting killed. Which would suck. Damn macho men, no wonder she'd always been careful to avoid them in the past. Sure it meant she was rarely satisfied with the easily-led-by-the-nose losers she occasionally hooked up with, but that was best for all concerned. Only, she hadn't realized that Ryan and Jacob would not be like that because she'd been very careful not to think about him. Them, she meant them. And not to dream about them. Well, him. She'd only dreamt about Ryan.

And, once again, she was avoiding the issue. She realized she was staring at her knees, having said nothing, when she had to look up at them through her lashes to gauge their mood. They were both watching her intently but didn't look angry at her lack of response.

In fact, they looked less angry than they had when she'd first seen them in her office.

A lie—a credible lie—was the only solution. She sat up straight and opened her mouth. Then closed it and slumped back down. *Shit, shit, shit.* She brought a hand to rub at her forehead. Great, now she was getting a headache. Five years on the run was more relaxing than she'd realized if this bit of stress was affecting her so strongly. It should be nothing compared to what she'd endured for so much of her life.

She sighed and rubbed her temple, allowing a small grimace. Now that she wasn't in panic mode, she had to remember that normal people expected a reaction, not the stony façade she'd perfected as a child.

"Look," she said finally. "It's not that complicated. I haven't stolen anything from your company or given data away, or planted bugs, or...whatever it is you think I've done."

Forcing herself to meet Jacob's eyes as best she could, she tried to convey the absolute truth of that. She wasn't sure if the pounding in her head was causing the nausea or the realization that she had seriously endangered these guys. If she couldn't convince them to let her go, soon, they were all going to be in a world of hurt. Which made meeting his eyes difficult.

"I admit I lied on my application. My name, my experience, hell, even my qualifications. But I was fully capable of doing the job, and I've worked my ass off to do it well. You don't even have to fire me. I quit. I'll leave—no harm, no foul."

She stood up, the ache in her head becoming a full throb. Dizziness had her swaying and she put a hand out to steady herself. Ryan caught her arm and lowered her to the couch before she had a chance to pull away. Jacob put his hand to her temple and she had time to think *that's weird* before darkness swamped her.

RYAN GAVE Jacob a worried glance but didn't voice his concerns. They'd been working together to penetrate the woman's maddeningly thick skull and he'd sensed Jacob's worry before she'd passed out. It wasn't normal for a human to be able to resist their mind search at all, let alone to the degree that Claire had. They should have stopped when she'd displayed signs of a headache, but had been convinced that once they were inside they could take away her pain. Only they hadn't gotten inside. Though focused on his mental efforts, Ryan had still heard every word she'd said. And they'd rung true but were so obviously a small part of the story that they hardly mattered. Her desire to escape was clear, and that did matter.

Jacob's eyes closed as he attempted to ease the pain they'd caused. Ryan rested one hand gently on her throat, letting her pulse point pull him in, careful to sense Claire's mental blocks rather than smash through them as they'd attempted to do before. They were damn solid. The pulse beneath his fingers calmed and she stirred.

He watched her face, so much more alive now, even in unconsciousness, than the blank expression she'd given them earlier. Why he'd found it so infuriating he had no idea. In the snap of a second her body went into full alert. Reacting on instinct he restrained her kicking legs while Jacob pulled her beating hands up over her head. Her eyes opened, wild with panic, and his heart clenched at the sight. She continued to fight and he had to practically lie on top of her to subdue her heaving body.

She blinked at him and her attempts to fight slowed as she realized where she was. He was absurdly pleased that she gave one final shudder and relaxed beneath him. At least some part of her trusted them and that made him all the more determined to find out what the hell was going on.

Chocolate and gold eyes watched him carefully as he forced himself to release her and back away, kneeling next to the couch. His dick ached at the loss of her softness and he considered the possibility of covering her back up in the very near future.

Her face was still tight with the pain of her headache and he got up to get her purse and a soda while Jacob handed her a tissue. She looked at it, confused, before he helped her to wipe a small smear of blood from beneath her nose. Shit, they really had done a number on her.

Refusing to feel too guilty and not wanting to dig through it again, he handed over her purse. She pulled out the small bottle of Tylenol and accepted the can of cola he offered. He sat next to her and Jacob resumed his seat across from them while they waited for her to wash down the pills.

When she leaned back against the couch, he wondered how much of the action was to rest and how much was to put some distance between them. He resisted the urge to scoot closer but reached out and rested a hand on her knee. Her thigh muscle tensed but he ignored that and used his thumb to make soothing circles. She wouldn't be able to keep it taut for long and he was touching her way too low to be accused of being inappropriate.

A light snort sounded in his head and he realized he'd broadcast that thought loudly enough for Jacob to hear. His mentor made no comment, however, and Claire's muscles slowly relaxed. When she didn't say anything, he glanced at Jacob.

Well? If we can't get in, how do we know she's telling the truth? he asked Jacob along the mental path they'd forged over the years.

You think she's lying?

No, but I don't know that she's not. Sometimes I wonder if we Fae have gotten too used to being able to read the humans' minds. They are forced to trust each other and us based on our actions, nothing more. Maybe our having to do the same for a change is a good reminder that the easy way is not always the best way.

Not sure how to respond to that, Ryan refocused his attentions on Claire. "Are you feeling better?" he asked.

"Yes, thank you."

She stared straight ahead and though her face was no longer tight with pain he wasn't sure how much he believed her. As Jacob had pointed out, he wasn't used to having to guess about such things. The calm expression gracing her face was too like the blank one she'd given them earlier. And pissed him off. Again.

"If you're through with your temper tantrum maybe you could answer our questions now."

He was glad to see her eyes widen at that. Then her chin lifted and she moved her knee out from under his hand. Since touching her hadn't helped with his ability to read her, he let her get away with it.

"You haven't asked me any questions that I haven't answered."

He could see from the amusement on Jacob's face that he was on his own for now.

"What's your name?"

"Claire Fiordalisi."

"You've already admitted you lied about your name on your application."

"It's my name right now."

He was pretty sure he managed to keep the growl from escaping his throat. "Fine. What was your name before that?"

"Sara Lancaster."

"And what was the name you were born with?" He had to unclench his teeth to get the sentence out, but somehow managed to keep from strangling her.

"None of your business."

"I think it is."

"I can't really help what you think."

"Maybe not, but you can't leave until I'm satisfied, either."

Her breath hitched at that and she glanced at the clock, her face paling. Was she supposed to be somewhere? Meet someone?

She took in a deep breath, which he recognized as a concession on her part. She was letting them see that she was tired and frustrated. Was she going to stop hiding? Stop pretending?

"All right, look. I didn't mean to be pissy, but like I said earlier, I lied about who I was but I did my best for this company. Nothing else matters. I'm going to leave. If someone comes looking for me, tell the truth. I was here one day and gone the next."

Her move to stand this time was slower, but when she gained her feet without any apparent dizziness she looked at him, then

Jacob. "I'm very sorry if my actions bring any trouble down on you, but it's best for all of us if I leave immediately."

She stepped around him and walked to the door, slinging her purse up on her shoulder.

He was beginning to wonder how much of the meek and compliant thing was an act. Sure, she'd come quietly when they'd gone to get her. She'd let him search her and been polite even when telling them to shove it. But her instinct when waking up had been to come up swinging and she'd sure managed to tell them essentially nothing so far, despite that acquiescent attitude.

When she reached the door, he held his breath, strangely eager for her reaction. She didn't disappoint.

No matter how much she pulled, the office door refused to budge. It wasn't locked, the knob turned freely and there was no deadbolt, but the door remained closed.

"Fuck! What part of 'I have to leave to keep you two asshats and your fucking company safe' do you not understand?"

Was that a snicker she heard? Whirling around she found both men right where she'd left them, faces solemn. She narrowed her eyes, too furious to guard her expression any longer. For fuck's sake, how was she supposed to keep them safe if they wouldn't let her go? Ryan, it had to be Ryan who'd laughed. He was trying too hard to look innocent.

She advanced on him, finger raised.

"I am trying—" She poked her finger into his chest. He raised his eyebrows at her. "To help you—" Another poke. "To keep you from becoming the target—" Poke. Poke. "Of some seriously deranged motherfuckers."

Tiny little crinkles appeared next to his perfect lips. He'd been pissed before, but now he was laughing at her? He'd better keep it inside or she was going to test her knee-to-testicle coordination.

Ryan's warm hand gently enfolded hers and brought her still-pointed finger to those damnable lips. Her eyes bugged out in shock as he laid a gentle kiss on the tip before bringing it back down and urging her whole hand to lay flat against his chest. His rock-hard chest. Wait, that wasn't the point. He—

"Careful. I don't want you to hurt yourself," he said, allowing a tiny smile to form.

Oh no, he didn't! "Arrrrggghhh."

Not exactly articulate, granted, but the phrase perfectly expressed her feelings at the moment. She tried to pull her hand free but he held firm.

Fine. On to plan B after all.

Careful not to telegraph her move, she brought her right knee up sharply. But she didn't connect with his gonads as she'd expected. Instead his other hand caught her neatly below the knee, which he moved to the side as he stepped in close. The sound of a throat clearing reminded her that Jacob was also in the room. Ryan didn't move, however, and she was unable to.

"As entertaining as this is," Jacob drawled with a hint of an accent she hadn't really noticed before, "perhaps we could get back to the matter at hand?"

Claire swallowed hard as Ryan let her leg drop, his hand running along her thigh, pressing it into his leg as she lowered it. She found herself practically straddling his leg, his hand on her ass, his hard cock pressing into her stomach.

Shit. Shit, shit, shit. She jerked back and he let her, though he held on until she was steady on her feet. Her breath was coming out hard and fast and she'd completely lost the ability to appear unaffected. If those chasing her had been present, she'd be toast right now. Even though she knew they weren't, her eyes darted around the room, convinced she would be punished somehow for her inattention.

She backed up, reaching the door once again, her eyes darting between Jacob, Ryan and Took. She knew it wouldn't open, but she tried the door once again. When it hit her back she nearly sobbed in relief. *Damn it, focus!* She needed to rein it in. Without another word to the men, she turned and walked out the door.

Refusing to give in to the instinct to run, she forced herself to keep a calm pace through the darkened corridors. She'd seen the clock in their office and been horrified to realize she'd been with them for over an hour. The fact that time had been slipping by and that every second in their presence was bringing danger closer and closer had jolted her back to reality. Now, seeing the evidence of that time gone by in the darkened offices reminded her that she'd let him distract her—*again*.

Damn it, they weren't going to be happy until she'd gotten them killed. Then what would she do? Could she live with more innocent lives on her conscience? Well, probably it wouldn't be an issue. At this point, if they got killed chances were good she'd already be dead. Or worse.

She reached the front counter and breezed past the security guard with a little wave.

"Good night, John."

"Good night, ma'am, Mr. Diel."

Claire almost tripped at that. A quick glance over her shoulder showed that Ryan was strolling along behind her, hands in his pockets. He gave a polite nod to John and she turned forward again. Son of a bitch, would this nightmare never end?

She was a little less than gentle as she pushed through the glass doors and out into the cool San Diego air. Having forced herself to live through a Michigan winter the previous year, she'd perhaps let the Southern California weather seduce her into staying here longer than she should have.

A sleek, black Mercedes with tinted windows pulled up as she made her way toward the parking lot. This time she did trip before stuttering to a stop. Ryan's hand on her back was probably meant to reassure her but all she could think was that he made a much bigger target than she did. The front passenger-side window rolled down and Took stuck his nose out.

"I am really beginning to hate you people," she muttered as Ryan urged her toward the car. Sure, she could scream and fight and run away, but that was clearly not going to gain her anything but unwanted attention. Conceding defeat, for now at least, she climbed into the car and scooted across the backseat when Ryan made to climb in behind her. She got as close to the other door and as far away from him as possible before pulling on her seat belt. When it clicked, she looked up and caught the dumb bastard looking quite pleased with himself.

"If someone was watching me, you're dead." She said it quietly, unable to raise the heat of anger.

He grinned. "I'm harder to kill than I look."

She just nodded. "Good luck with that, then."

She spent the rest of the ride watching out the window as Jacob drove them to a neighborhood she hadn't bothered to visit, knowing she would stick out like a sore thumb amongst the wealthy homeowners. Jacob, on the other hand, looked the part, and she wondered if he'd grown up with money, or if this was all due to his success. Since she'd been with the company, she'd not heard of him dating, so he must be discreet. No way were women—or men?—not throwing themselves at the handsome bachelor. He carried himself like an aristocrat, and even his longer-than-corporate hair looked handsomely old-fashioned, not rebellious. His stunning blue eyes and sharp cheekbones should have made him pretty, but the fact that they graced a strong face and body made him gorgeous.

Watching his profile, she wondered why he hadn't been the one appearing in her dreams, instead of his cocky partner. He was older, but not so much that he was out of her range. He was built, clearly took care of himself, and she was one-hundred-percent sure he knew how to take care of a lady. Maybe that was the problem. She'd certainly never classified herself as a lady.

They went through a security gate and up a long drive. The house appeared isolated, though she knew there were neighbors not too far away. At least she didn't have to worry about the security—that was one thing she knew these guys excelled at.

Jacob pulled into a garage and got out of the car but Claire couldn't seem to summon the energy to do the same. Ryan leaned over and popped her seat belt open but she just looked at him. His amusement was gone, so she didn't have to hit him, which was good. She had nothing left for the day. Her door opened and Took stuck his furry face into hers and offered her a lick.

"Took, be a gentleman." Jacob pulled the huge dog back and offered her a hand. She took it, only then realizing that her headache had gone. At least there was that.

"Welcome to my home."

"You shouldn't have brought me here." Her voice sounded tired to her. Had she given up? Wasn't she supposed to be a tough bitch? A bit of arguing and a headache and she was all done-in? Apparently so.

Jacob tucked her hand into his elbow and led her into the house. She should be examining the layout, evaluating the exits, studying the security, but what was the point? They were security specialists, and damn good ones. She wasn't leaving until they let her. There was no point wasting her time. She let him bring her to a door and just waited while he went inside, turning on lights and drawing back the bedcovers. It was a lovely guest room done in soothing shades of brown and blue. The bed looked to be about as comfortable and inviting as a bed had ever looked to her.

She heard Ryan come up behind her, though he didn't touch.

"Why don't you take a nap while we get dinner ready," he suggested, his voice low and soothing.

Apparently she looked as shitty as she felt if they were treating her like a frail guest rather than an incarcerated suspect. Whatever, as long as they left her alone with that bed, she'd worry about the rest later. Her feet brought her into the room with no conscious input from her brain.

"Bathroom is through there." Jacob pointed. "And here are some comfortable clothes you can change into." He gestured behind her to Ryan who was setting what looked like sweats and a t-shirt on the dresser. They walked out, closing the door behind them.

Within two minutes she'd removed her flats, nylons, skirt, blouse and bra, visited the bathroom, washed her face and donned the t-shirt before sliding under the covers. While she was vulnerable to the two men who'd brought her here, she was sure that she was safe from attack here. For now, that would have to be enough. And didn't that just piss her off more—that she trusted them not to hurt her in her sleep, but was putting them in danger by leading her enemies to them. If they died because of her, she would deserve whatever fate befell her.

CHAPTER TWO

Jacob led the way to his study and Ryan didn't need to see his partner's face to know the other man was amused. His suspicions were confirmed when Jacob turned to hand him a whiskey, not even trying to hide his grin.

"I fail to see how this situation is amusing. She's keeping huge secrets from us. Probably dangerous secrets."

Jacob waved his hand, unconcerned. "We'll get to all that. In the meantime, it's nice to see a woman who doesn't fall all over herself to please you. You get too much of that, from humans and Fae alike."

"That's not true. Plenty of women aren't interested in me."

His partner just raised an eyebrow over his drink. Jacob sat on the couch, Took settling in at his feet while Ryan paced back and forth before the empty fireplace.

"Whatever. How women react to me is not what's at issue here. We need to talk about Claire. How did we just spend two hours with her and get no answers to our questions?" he fumed.

"We did not actually ask very many questions," Jacob reminded him.

Ryan stopped pacing long enough to glare.

"She's obviously in trouble and needs help. Why doesn't she ask us for help? It's what we do!"

"She doesn't know that we're here to ensure the safety of humans from the Fae that do not wish them well."

"But she does know that we run a security company, damn it."

"I think she's been running for a very long time."

Ryan sighed and dropped into a chair. He held his glass to his forehead. "We hurt her."

"We made a mistake," Jacob agreed. "We'll fix it by helping her."

"Whether she wants it or not."

Jacob stood. "Come, let's make her a meal. She'll wake up hungry."

As they worked together with the ease of longtime partners, Ryan reflected on what they'd learned. Jacob had been alerted to a hacker attempting to gain access to their computer system earlier that day and had immediately diverted the hacker to a dummy system in place for just that purpose. Jacob had worked with their head computer specialist to track the hacker while Ryan had looked into what the hacker was after.

The search had been for any females employed with the company less than nine months. There were two and he'd examined both of their employee files. Claire Fiordalisi's had passed the company's initial screening but a careful look had found flaws. He'd be having a word with the supervisor who'd approved the file—and that word would be "fired". Convinced that they had a spy in their midst, he and Jacob had left the computer expert in charge of tracking down the hacker while they'd gone to take care of Miss Fiordalisi.

"You seem to be reacting to her quite strongly," Jacob said as Ryan returned from setting the table.

"I wouldn't put it that way."

"Ah. How would you put it?"

"Don't tell me you weren't frustrated that she didn't tell us what was going on."

Jacob quirked one eyebrow at Ryan, which never failed to annoy him.

"She's in danger of some kind and has brought it down on our company. We have a responsibility to our employees to protect them."

"Of course."

"This is what we do. We could probably have the whole situation resolved in an hour if she would just fess up." Ryan put the silverware down on the table with a crack.

"Do you think so?"

"Of course. Don't you?"

"I find that I trust her not to have run from anything so small and inconsequential that it could be easily fixed, even by you or me."

"Hmph."

Of course, with the resources at their disposal, it wouldn't take too long to figure out who she was and what problems plagued her. But he wanted to know now, and he wanted her to trust him enough to tell him herself.

The oven timer beeped and Jacob picked up potholders. "Would you like to finish this while I wake her? It should be ready to eat in about fifteen minutes and I'm sure she'd like a minute to refresh herself."

Ryan didn't answer, just turned and left the kitchen. He reminded himself that he wasn't annoyed with Jacob. He wasn't even really annoyed with Claire. Just with the situation. She needed help and he was in a position to help her, if she would just trust them. He ran a hand through his hair and noted that he needed to get it cut. Of course, he could just use magic, but he preferred doing most things the human way. It kept him in touch with the world that he was living in.

He paused outside her door to gather himself. He wasn't used to swinging through such a wide range of emotions in such a short period of time. Pure anger at the idea that an employee had been seeking to do harm to the company. Puzzled frustration when they couldn't read Claire and therefore couldn't resolve the situation easily. Fear when they'd inadvertently hurt her and still hadn't been able to break through. Compassion— where had that come from? Surely he was smart enough not to fall for a sob story. Hell, she hadn't even gotten around to telling them a sob story. Lust. Well, it was best not to think about that one right now while she was just beyond the door, snuggled up in the bed that he used when staying at Jacob's house.

A soft knock and a half-second pause were all the warning he gave before opening the door quietly. He carefully didn't acknowledge to himself the desire to see her at peace again.

She lay in the middle of the bed, curled up into a small ball, Took a huge presence at her back. Well, that was very interesting. Jacob had spelled all the doors to open for Took but he was surprised that the dog had already allied himself with the girl. Her hideous straw-like black hair lay drab against the pillow. Her head was tucked down so that he could barely see her face. Creamy skin kissed by a small spattering of freckles reminded him of the flush that had graced her cheeks when he'd been caught staring at her legs.

He eased a finger to move her hair back from her forehead but stopped, remembering how she'd come up swinging the last time she'd woken up. He wasn't worried she'd hurt him, but she didn't need another hard awakening today. Instead, he called a slight breeze to blow across her face, imbuing it with a touch of his scent.

Her chest rose, taking in a deep lungful, and she stirred then froze. Because she realized she was in a strange bed or because she realized she wasn't alone?

"Claire."

"Ryan."

He was absurdly pleased she knew who it was. "Dinner will be ready in a couple of minutes."

"I'll be right out." Her body moved under the covers, stretching, but she didn't look at him, didn't open her eyes.

Without conscious thought, he reached his hand and brushed her hair back farther from her face, though his breeze had already done the job. She didn't move as he traced his finger along her hairline down to her ear before tucking the strands in place. The rough texture of her hair against the smooth softness of her skin offended him. He had to squelch the desire to restore the overdyed locks to their original state so that he could see how she was meant to look.

Eyes still closed, she turned her head toward him, into his hand. He cupped her cheek and brushed his thumb over the bruised flesh under her eyes. When had she last had a good rest?

"Is your headache gone?" he asked.

"Yes." She swallowed, then turned her head away from him. "I'll be right out."

Ryan left, Took following. They stood outside the closed door and listened to the rustling of sheets and the rush of water. When footsteps approached the door he moved back, leaning against the wall.

Her wary expression smoothed into blankness when she caught sight of him. This time, instead of pissing him off, compassion washed through him, as well as curiosity. He wanted to know who she was and how she'd come to be that person. He wanted to know her, inside and out.

Pushing away from the wall, he turned and walked to the dining room instead of pulling her into his arms and testing the softness of her lips. That time was coming. He would see to it.

CLAIRE DEBATED WORKING up a mad again. Fear and anger were so useful for getting things done. But right now her options seemed to be limited to sitting in the guest bedroom or joining the guys for dinner. Since she was hungry and they most likely wouldn't let her hide in the bedroom alone anyway, she followed Ryan into the dining room.

Her mistakes were clear. First, she never should have applied for the job at Teck Security. Second, she should have left as soon as she'd found herself enjoying the comfortable, friendly atmosphere and started having midnight fantasies about Ryan Diel. And afternoon fantasies. And evening fantasies. Third, she should have figured out a way to get out of the office as soon as they'd come for her. Although she still had no clue how she might have managed that. Lastly, she should not be letting herself feel safe and damn-near relaxed with them. She needed to figure out what they wanted to hear that would convince them to let her go and get on with her life, far away from them.

Spicy marinara and garlic scents wafted down the hall. It smelled delicious and gave her an idea. She hated formal dinners. It brought to mind too many memories of her childhood. Being forced to sit around the table together as if they were the happy family unit from a classic television show. It had been a frightening experience, knowing that one wrong word or look could set off the volatile group. She would use those memories as she'd always used them, to shore up her defenses and keep this sudden and disturbing tendency to relax around Ryan and Jacob at bay.

The room they turned into was perfect. Gorgeous walnut table with seating for twelve. A crystal chandelier casting subdued lighting over the elegant place settings grouped around the near end. Soft music breezing through the room, adding a background that wouldn't interfere with conversation. It was everything she'd hoped it would be, everything she hated most when eating a meal—there was no chance she'd relax and lose her resolve.

Jacob slid out a chair and she sat. Her palms grew damp as she took the linen napkin from the place setting and draped it over her sweats-clad thighs. Her stomach lurched knowing she could be beaten for wearing such inappropriate clothing to the dinner table. She stared at the large bowl of pasta in front of her, her hands folded on her lap, waiting to see what would happen next.

"Are you feeling better?" Jacob asked, placing a salad bowl next to her.

"Yes, thank you." She scooped up what she hoped was the right portion and placed it carefully on her plate, then passed the bowl back to Jacob, who sat to her right. Across from her Ryan was adding sauce to the pasta he'd already served himself. She watched so that she could repeat the process. Pasta had never been served this way in her house. A tiny scoff in the back of her head that they wouldn't be offended if she chose her portions incorrectly was quickly shoved aside.

"I hope you were able to get some rest." Jacob offered her the garlic bread once she'd added sauce to her pasta.

"I'll pass, thank you. And yes, I got some rest, thank you for asking."

Ryan and Jacob exchanged a look. She knew she was confusing them, but as long as they weren't angry, that was fine with her.

There was a wineglass in front of her, already filled with a luscious-looking red, but she bypassed it and picked up the water glass. Grandfather would be insulted to have his wine selection dismissed, but she needed some food in her system before she risked it. Her tuna-salad-sandwich lunch was a long-distant memory.

A quick glance at the two men—without making eye contact—confirmed that they were ready to eat, only waiting for her. She picked up her fork and stabbed it into a piece of lettuce and mushroom. The tangy Italian dressing helped force the bite down. *Crap.* She really was out of practice. For years she'd sat through the dreaded family dinners. Now she wasn't sure she would make it through this one meal with two people who didn't really scare her. Apparently she was channeling her childhood a little too well. Her purpose had been to distance herself from the overly helpful pair, not constrict her throat in terror or turn her stomach with nausea.

But that's just what was happening as her eyes returned to the basket of garlic bread. She hadn't been able to eat the stuff for years, though it had once been a favorite. It only took one dinner gone wrong, a dinner that ended with someone's blood pooling onto the plate of bread, to put an end to that particular treat.

Another sip of water would help. She reached her hand out and was horrified to see her fingers shaking as they wrapped around the glass. Damn it, she could do better. Had to do better. Ice clinked as she brought the glass to her lips.

A sudden bang as Ryan dropped his fists to the table had her jerking before she could freeze herself. She let only her eyes move as her gaze flew to his face to see what the problem was and how she needed to react. He was staring at her. Was that anger? Her breathing picked up but she tried to keep it from being obvious. Eyes on his, she carefully set the glass down and waited for some clue as to what she should do. Movement from her right had her already tense muscles screaming for action but she clamped down and remained still.

Jacob's hand came to rest on Ryan's arm. Ryan looked away from her and over to Jacob. Claire allowed her head to turn just enough that she could see them both. Neither spoke but Ryan took a deep breath and seemed to relax. Slowly—very, very slowly— she let herself remember that she was not in her family's home, not at the family dinner table. She was with Ryan and Jacob. She couldn't say she trusted them, but they'd given her no reason to think they would harm her.

Guilt washed through her. She hadn't realized she would fall back into the old fears quite so deeply. She closed her eyes and let the tension drain from her. It took more strength than she would have guessed but she forced her head up to look Jacob in the eyes.

"I'm sorry. Would you mind so much if we ate somewhere else?"

She didn't know what he was thinking as he studied her, but he rose.

"Of course. I rarely use this room, as I seldom have guests. There's a much cozier breakfast nook that I usually use. Why don't we go there?"

Swallowing against her suddenly tight throat, Claire rose, picking up her plate and glass.

It took two trips before they had everything transferred to the lovely nook off Jacob's kitchen. Instead of blocking her into the middle of the bench seat, Jacob pulled a chair from against the wall and sat opposite her. She wasn't sure she could suppress her relief so she picked up her wineglass and hid behind it.

Jacob's sigh suggested he wasn't unaware of her hiding.

"I think it's time you told us what's going on," he said.

She put down her glass and nudged the basket of garlic bread closer to Ryan so she didn't have to look at it.

"Fine. I grew up with bad people. Monsters. I chose to leave and they're not happy about that, so I need to stay hidden. Simple. It's best to stay ahead of them, trust me, so I'll just leave here and you don't have to worry about me, or them, anymore."

"Monsters?" Ryan glanced at Jacob in surprise before returning his attention to her. "Demons?"

She blinked at him. "Uh. No. Murderers. Rapists. Thieves."

"Ah." He sat back with a smile. "We can help you with that." He resumed eating.

Fear for them tried to intrude but she pulled on her anger instead. "No, you can't. And you won't. You'll stay out of it. Stay safe. Stay away from me."

Ryan just waved his fork at her, his mouth too full to answer.

Crossing her arms over her chest she leaned back and glared at him.

His confidence should piss her off. Did piss her off. Too bad it was also sexy as hell. A man shouldn't look sexy eating spaghetti, damn it.

"Let me be very clear. I'm not asking for your help. I don't want it. The only thing I need from you is to let me walk away. And if you don't, you won't just have the monsters to deal with, you'll have me. If I wouldn't put up with being ordered around and kept in place by the people who made me, you can sure as hell bet I won't put up with it from you."

"Of course you can leave, if you want to," Jacob said. Ryan opened his mouth as if to object, but remained silent. "I would appreciate it, though, if you would tell us your family's name, so that we might be prepared," Jacob added.

She looked back and forth between them but neither seemed concerned. Her well-developed sense of the truth told her that Jacob meant what he'd said. So, okay, they were just going to let her go. That was good. Right.

"I'll think about it." She tucked back into her dinner. She'd need all the good fuel she could get as she started on the next phase of her life. And the wine didn't hurt, either.

Jacob managed to get them chatting casually while they finished the meal, then brought out ice cream and all the fixings for sundaes. She was too tired to be more than mildly amused that the elegant man kept such items on hand. Pouring heated caramel sauce over the French vanilla ice cream, she caught Ryan's intent gaze as he added chocolate to his own. A sudden vision of him licking the sauce from her breasts rose in her mind. Her breath caught at the vivid image and she forced her attention back to her hands, righting the jar and placing it back on the table. Ryan picked up the can of whipped cream and slowly leaned over to dispense a long layer of creamy goodness into her bowl.

She refused to meet his eyes as she picked up the maraschino cherries and spooned a couple from the jar. What the hell, she would only have this one night with him, maybe she should give in to the heat that was building between them. Though he wasn't her usual type, there was no denying that he made her body ache. A sprinkle of nuts finished off the sundae and she picked up the bowl and moved to the living room.

A fire crackled and she headed for that, taking a seat on the raised hearth. Jacob followed her in, sitting on the large leather sofa. When Ryan joined them he moved straight toward her, sitting close enough that the heat from his thigh rivaled that of the fire. She considered giving him a good death glare before changing seats but decided she would be spiting herself more than him. The truth was she liked the feel of him next to her. She relaxed her body, letting her leg fall slightly closer to his.

The first bite of the sundae was perfect, just the right combination of ice cream and toppings. She closed her eyes and savored the treat. Her mind wandered back to the vision of Ryan licking sauce from her breasts and she moaned around the delicious coldness.

Ryan shifted restlessly next to her and she suppressed a smile. *Oh yeah.* One night with him would carry her through years of the dishrags she usually limited herself to. Her nipples tightened at the idea. Another cold spoonful did little to counteract the heat that was consuming her body. Next to her, Ryan was shoveling in his sundae at an alarming rate. Hiding a smile, she slowed her own pace even more, letting the spoon slide out ever so slowly between her lips, eyes closing again to fully appreciate the deliciousness.

The clatter of bowl hitting hearth made her heart beat faster but she maintained her pace, bringing another spoonful to her lips. Her eyes opened slightly when Ryan leaned into her, bracing a hand against her back. She angled the spoon toward him and he parted his lips. She made sure to get cream on his lip before allowing him to draw the spoon inside. His eyes were hot on her, full of intent and promise. A shiver raced up her spine and he pressed his hand harder into her back, his thumb taking up a circular caress.

She pulled the spoon back and he swallowed before darting his tongue out to clean the mess she'd made. Was it intentional that he left the bit at the slightly pointed bow? She hoped so. Leaning forward, she darted her own tongue out to catch the speck of whipped cream. A tiny growl came from him as she pulled back. He tightened his arm, holding her close.

"Are we going to do this?" His breath whispered against her lips. "If you want me to leave, tell me now."

She put her hand on his thigh and slowly inched it up, eyes steady on his, lips a breath apart. Angling her hand in, she found her prize. He caught his breath as she palmed his length, hard and growing harder.

"You won't stop me from leaving in the morning?"

"I won't stop you."

"You would walk away, right now?" she asked, dismayed to sound so breathless. Damn it, she was going for saucy and in control. To compensate, she squeezed, hard.

"Only if you asked me to." He brought a hand up to her cheek, a gentle caress that had her heart clenching.

But it wasn't her heart that she wanted clenching so she closed the tiny distance between them and captured his mouth with hers.

She wanted hot, hard, fast. Now. He tasted of chocolate sauce and vanilla and met her demanding kiss thrust for thrust. Her hands scrabbled at his shirt, desperate to find a way inside and feel bare skin. He stood, pulling her up with him, then lifted her so her legs came naturally around his waist. His obvious strength should have frightened her, but she could only be thankful as he stalked out of the room, never backing away from the kiss that threatened to consume her.

Buttons gave way at last and he gasped as her hands, chilled from the ice-cream bowl, met his warm flesh. She pulled back and glanced over his shoulder as they left the room, only now remembering that they hadn't been alone. But the room was empty and she let all thoughts of their host vanish as Ryan reclaimed her mouth.

She closed her eyes and abandoned his chest to thread her fingers through his hair and hold him closer, though he'd made no move to back away. She explored his mouth, his tongue dancing and flirting with hers as he let her before boldly switching places. Had she ever felt a kiss with her entire body? Her nipples tightened and ached for contact. Her stomach fluttered and her pussy contracted. More, she needed more.

Ryan broke the kiss and the world tilted, but since she found herself landing and bouncing on a bed, she forgave him. He stood at the side, watching her. His open shirt framed a chest that she wanted to spend an hour exploring. Hard planes and the sprinkling of hair invited her touch, preferably with lips and tongue.

She would have moved to do just that but he stalled her with a hand on her bare feet. He gave a small caress then gripped the legs of the sweats and yanked. The baggy pants gave easily and she found herself half-naked, her plain cotton underpants pulled low down one hip but stubbornly clinging to the other.

With the careful planning that she prided herself on, despite the evidence from the activities of the day to the contrary, as she rose up on her elbows to get a better view, her large t-shirt was caught under her elbows and pulled tight across her breasts.

"Gorgeous," he murmured as he slid his hands slowly up her legs.

Too slowly. Abandoning her pose, she pulled the t-shirt over her head and tossed it aside.

RYAN FROZE his advance when Claire suddenly sat up and ripped her shirt off before reaching for his belt buckle. He let her push his pants down then kicked them away, but grabbed her hands when she reached for his cock. If she touched him it would be over before she knew it. Watching her eat her ice cream had pushed him close to the edge, but he had no intention of letting her push him over before he had her good and ready.

Holding her hands tight to the bed he climbed up, framing her legs with his. She pushed up and he met her with a kiss. He tried for slow and sweet but she was having none of it. She yanked and he released her. Her hands found his back and drew fine scratches as far as she could reach. Heat flared through his body. Bracing himself on one arm, he reached down with the other to test her readiness. The slight shield of cotton was soaked and he ran his finger up her slit until her hips arched off the bed as he found her clit.

Her ragged moan almost undid him. All right, slow and sweet was obviously not going to happen here. Next time, he promised himself, he could take the time to savor. Right now she obviously needed him as a badly as he needed her. Together they pulled her panties down. She reached for him again but he evaded her hands and lowered his mouth to her pussy. Her hands found his hair as he swiped up her cream with his tongue.

"Mmmmm," he growled, smiling when the vibrations had her moaning.

"Ryan—" Whatever she was going to say was lost as he moved to her clit and sucked it between his teeth.

He lashed it with his tongue before releasing it with a tiny kiss. "Do you like that, Claire?"

"Fuck me, Ryan. Fuck me now."

Her fingers in his hair gripped tighter and his cock jerked as he pushed his tongue inside her. She bucked against him. He looked up and found her head thrown back and eyes closed. Beautiful, she was so beautiful. He wanted to watch her come apart in his arms. Surging up her body, found her mouth, shared the taste of her. She wrapped her legs tight around him, holding him close as her tongue dueled with his.

He pushed a finger inside her. Goddess, she was so tight. He added another finger and angled them, searching for the right spot. Her muscles clenched around him and she gasped into his mouth. He tapped and was rewarded with more cream easing his way. She broke the kiss, pushing hard on his shoulder and he let her roll them over, his fingers slipping free. If she wanted to ride him, he had no problem with that. He spelled a condom into his hand, hoping she wouldn't notice that it hadn't been there a minute before, and handed it to her.

Her hands shook a little in her eagerness to sheath him and he had to force himself to stay still and not rush her. Finally she was ready. With one hand braced against his abs, she used the other to hold his cock steady and lowered herself. He watched her face, eyes closed in pleasure and concentration. When he breached her, she paused, breathing hard.

He reached forward but she wasn't paying much attention to him right now. The hand holding him steady squeezed as she came down farther, her inner muscles pulling him in. He should be insulted that she hardly seemed aware of whose dick she was impaling herself on, but the tiny gasps, the fingers clenching against his chest, the careful, almost fearful look on her face made that impossible. It was as if she feared that the pleasure would end at any second. There was no chance of that, he would see to it.

Bringing his hands to her thighs, he helped support her weight. Her shiver at his touch brought a grin to his face. Good thing her eyes were closed or she probably would have taken that as some kind of challenge. She let go of his dick and braced that hand against his chest as well, lowering herself the final distance. It took a great deal of his strength to remain still, but he managed it. After a second, she began to move.

Again, he had the idea that he should be insulted—it was almost as if he was a piece of equipment that she was using for her pleasure. But he got the distinct impression that she hadn't allowed herself this pleasure in a long time, if ever. She raised herself up and down a couple times, then added a swirl that brought a gasp to both their lips.

"Ryan." She opened her eyes at last. Glazed with pleasure, they pierced his soul. She knew exactly who she was with.

He ran his hands up her sides and cupped her breasts. They filled his hands and he squeezed gently, gratified when her head fell back with another moan. Her rhythm increased, up, down, up, down with a twist. He wasn't sure how long he could last, was horrified to feel his balls drawing up already. What was it about this maddening woman that made him lose control so quickly? Well, he could live with it for now, as long as he could return the favor. He took a nipple in each hand and pinched. She gave a cross between and groan and a squeal, her back arching, her pace faltering, her nails digging into his flesh as she came in a small rush.

When her eyes met his they glinted in challenge. A smile spread across her face, so genuine with its hint of mischief that his heart stuttered. He had a feeling such smiles were rare for her, and he wanted to see more.

Claire sat more fully upright, bringing her hands up from his chest to knock his aside. She cupped her own breasts, pushing them together, flicking her nipples, all while grinding against his groin and squeezing her inner muscles tight.

He let a groan escape but retaliated by sliding his hands up her thighs, curving them in, closer and closer to where their bodies joined. Her ragged breathing hitched as his thumbs carefully pulled her pussy lips apart. They both stared down as she rose, revealing his slick cock. She lifted almost all the way off, and met his eyes. They moved as one. He arched up as she slammed down. Eyes locked, they did it again and again, both determined to send the other over first.

Ryan brought one hand up to reclaim her luscious breast. She let him, but moved her hand down, reaching behind her to find his balls.

"Ah, fuck! Claire!"

He erupted and was relieved to feel her convulse around him. She collapsed against him and he managed to bring his arms around her. They were both slick with sweat, panting heavily, and he wasn't sure he'd ever been more satisfied in his life. And he didn't even know her real name.

The idea of letting her walk away tomorrow made him very uneasy. He'd almost protested when Jacob had promised her she could leave in the morning. He'd told himself that it was simply his responsibility to her kind that objected so strongly. He was on this plane to protect humans, and she was a human who needed protecting. And loving, apparently, as he'd managed to get her into his bed less than five hours after first speaking with her. But that didn't mean there was more to it than basic attraction.

Oh Goddess, the attraction. Despite the ugly mess of her hair, she was very attractive. Her creamy skin was pale in the darkness. The covers hid the curves that felt so good against his body, but he well remembered what they'd looked like in her proper business skirt and blouse. Hell, even in his too-large sweats and t-shirt her body had tempted him to distraction. Her brown eyes were flecked liberally with gold, a combination he wouldn't have thought possible in a human. He supposed that technically he'd seen more attractive women, been with more attractive women. So maybe it was her attitude, as frustrating as it was, that was so damn sexy. It wasn't often that a human, male or female, stood up to two Fae warriors as she had.

How could she be so infuriating and so attractive at the same time? He should just go fix the problem with her family and leave her to live her life in a peace that she hadn't yet experienced. Who knew what kind of person she would be if she were able to live a normal, safe life? He could give her that, then move on. Just like he always did.

She snuggled into him a bit more and her warm breath caressed his skin. He risked a bit more magic to dispose of the condom, tightened his hold on her and joined her in sleep.

CHAPTER THREE

Claire woke up determined to put this episode behind her and start her next identity. She wasn't usually in such a good mood between lives, but how could she not be after last night? She ignored the tiny part of her that wondered what it would be like to stay here, to continue to live *this* life. To keep Claire. But the truth was that if she hadn't been planning on leaving, she never would have given in to the attraction to Ryan, so it wouldn't have been the same. Better that she enjoyed the hell out of that brief interlude and moved on.

Still, part of her hesitated to roll out of the comfortable bed, made more so by the arms wrapped around her. How often did she get to feel so...content? Even more rare than sleeping with a guy was actually *sleeping* with a guy. She heaved a deep breath and rolled free of his arms, suppressing a smile when he gave an irritated grunt. It wouldn't do her any good to get used to this.

She started the shower and wasn't at all surprised when Ryan appeared naked at the door, a hopeful look on his face.

"Are you going to give me any trouble about leaving today?" she asked him, opening the door and watching the steam billow around him.

He narrowed his eyes at her but then sighed. "No."

Taking a step back, she invited him in with a smile. He made a noise as he entered that sounded a lot like a growl. She cocked her eyebrow which made him growl—yes, that was definitely the sound—louder. Her answer started out a laugh but turned into a squeal as he grabbed her hips and brought her against his body. His fingers had to grip tightly against her slippery wet skin and she wondered if she would bruise. She'd never hoped to before, never hoped to have marks to remind her of a lover.

He backed her against the wall, the tile cold until her skin warmed it, though she hardly noticed as his mouth descended toward hers. Last night he'd tried to be tender, but she'd demanded rough. Now there was no effort on his part for easy—he was taking her, hard and fast. As his tongue mated with hers, he thrust his hips forward. His hard cock pressed into her stomach and she reached down to grab his ass and press him even closer. The sound he made this time sent a shiver through her body that had nothing to do with being cold.

He threaded his fingers through her wet hair, allowing her no movement. It should annoy her. It should scare her. It only made her hotter. She let her nails dig into his skin, just a bit. He squeezed his leg between hers, pressing his thigh up into her pussy. A gasp escaped her into his mouth and he finally pulled back, watching her as he repeated the move.

"You like that, Claire?"

"Yeah. Yeah, that's good, you can keep doing that." She forced the words out though they didn't sound as strong as she'd like.

He smiled and let his leg drop. "Are you in a hurry to leave this morning?" His thumbs caressed her temples and he wore a shit-eating grin. Suddenly the hands in her hair didn't feel good. They felt confining. The teasing warmth slid from her body, replaced by a wave of cold steel. She let the transition show plainly on her face, in her eyes. He saw and understood, his own expression going from superior masculinity to confused irritation.

Fine, he could be irritated, but if he didn't let her go, he was going to be in pain too.

"Let me go."

He studied her for precisely one second less than she was willing to give him, then took a step back, pulling his fingers free from her hair with a last small caress against her cheeks.

"Is that what this is? You think if the sex is hot enough, I'll just stay?" He opened his mouth to respond, but she kept going. "You want me to stay that badly, that you'd whore yourself out to make it happen?"

An ugly red flushed over his face and he took another step back. He studied her, then turned and left the shower. Bracing her hands against the wall she ducked her head under the spray. It didn't help. A quick twist of the knob made the water almost cold. That didn't really help, either, but it got her moving. She washed quickly and was drying off within a couple of minutes. It was long enough to have her second-guessing the situation. Had she been unnecessarily harsh?

Her early life had been all about protecting herself *from* those around her, those who wished to use her. Her later life had been about *protecting* those around her, innocents who could so easily be dragged into the fray. Keeping her distance was the only constant, and damn it, he *had* crossed the line.

She wrapped one towel around her hair and the other around her body and went into the bedroom to find her clothes. They'd disappeared but a pair of jeans and a t-shirt were laid out on the bed. She bent over and towel-dried her hair, then reached for the clothes.

The jeans looked as if they would fit her fine, which gave her a flash of amusement at how well the guys had judged her size. The t-shirt, however, was—interesting. It was dark green, fitted and emblazoned with Tinkerbell. Well, maybe not emblazoned exactly, but it looked as if the small fairy would sit right between her breasts. Also, it looked as if there was—she poked a finger at the shirt—yes, glitter. So not something Claire would ever wear. In fact, not one of the identities she'd assumed in the last five years had ever worn a cartoon character of any kind.

What the hell did Ryan mean by leaving this for her? Why would Jacob have a shirt like this in his house? As their employee she'd worn blouses and proper skirts or slacks. She pulled on the jeans while staring at the t-shirt laying on the bed. When she couldn't put it off any longer, she pulled the shirt over her head and looked in the mirror.

Ridiculous. Totally ridiculous. And cute. Which was absolutely not appropriate for trying to stay anonymous. She slipped on the simple sneakers, which fit perfectly.

A soft knock on the door interrupted her thoughts and she braced herself for confrontation.

"Come in." Her tone wasn't very inviting, but so be it.

The door opened and Ryan stood there, his hands in the front pockets of his jeans, his posture apologetic.

"I didn't mean it like that."

She cocked her eyebrow at him and he scowled.

"Not really. I mean, I would rather you didn't leave, but it's not like I would have stopped, unless you'd asked me to."

He seemed sincere but it hardly mattered at this point. It was past time for her to go and it would be easier if they weren't basking in the afterglow. She shrugged, careful to imbue it with just the right amount of nonchalance, then smirked as his gaze tracked down to the fairy riding on her chest.

"Fine. I appreciate your telling me that. I'll be out of here in just a minute." She grabbed her purse and pulled a brush from it, yanking it through her tangles more sharply than she'd intended.

"Claire," he began, blinking his way back up to meet her eyes.

"It's fine, Ryan. It's over. Last night was great." She sighed and let her voice soften. She didn't want to hurt him. "It was fantastic, actually." His scowl softened into more of a frown. "But that doesn't change anything. I have to go, and you promised that you wouldn't stop me." Detangled, she tossed the brush into her purse and slung the bag over her shoulder, finally turning to face him head-on.

"Fine." He backed away from the door and motioned for her to lead the way. Took was waiting behind him and she stopped to give the huge dog a good ear rub. Maybe someday things would settle down and she could get a dog. The thought had her stomach cramping. Took woofed at her as if to ask her what was wrong. She pressed a hand to her middle and turned her back on him. No, she wouldn't have a dog. Not ever again.

Jacob stepped out of a room she hadn't been in yet. "Good morning, Claire. Do you think we could talk for a bit before you leave?"

She didn't even try to hide her displeasure. "What would be the point, Jacob? I will be leaving this morning. Nothing you say will change that."

"I understand. I merely wanted to get some information from you so that Ryan and I can adequately protect our people."

Okay, so he already knew which buttons to push with her. Great. At least he was better at it than Ryan. "Fifteen minutes, no more." She made the effort to sound rude. Jacob's old-world manners made it hard, but she managed.

He bowed his head at her and backed up, gesturing her into the room. His study, she supposed. It was comfortably furnished, masculine and enduring. Actually, it was a lot like her grandfather's study, but where that room had always felt like a purchased affectation for the man who'd grown up poor, this room felt natural and comfortable. She took the seat he indicated on the couch, relieved when Ryan didn't join her, choosing instead to lean against the heavy desk.

"You were considering giving us some information about your fam—the people after you. I promise you that we are good enough at our jobs to make some inquiries and determine the best way to protect our employees without letting them know that we're looking," Jacob said.

Her shoulders slumped in defeat but she managed not to bitch out loud. She had told them she'd think about it, but hadn't devoted a single second to the subject. Carefully not glancing at what had distracted her all night, she gave Jacob a nod. In this, she would trust them. If they weren't good enough to do as he'd said, then there wasn't much she could do about it. But she wouldn't walk away leaving them blind.

"The core of it is my family. The Smiths." She wasn't surprised by Ryan's amused grunt. "I'm sure Grandfather changed his name to Smith at some point, I have no idea what his birth name was. But Fred Smith—yes, his name was Fred, apparently his parents didn't realize that they were raising a psychopathic murderer, so they didn't realize they couldn't name him Fred—dragged himself out of a poor upbringing by being an evil bastard. He stole and killed, threatened and terrorized. Now he's semiretired, meaning he runs the family, but doesn't have much to do with the daily running of the business. He leaves that to my mother, and my uncle. Uncle John—" She paused for Ryan's outright laughter. "Is more interested in hurting people than running a business, so he and my mother make a great team. Not that she minds hurting people, she just prefers to not sweat while doing so, and is happy to sit back and watch someone else do the actual work of it. Anyway, they live in Northern Florida."

"What's your name?" Ryan asked.

She finally looked at him and was surprised at the serious expression he wore. "It doesn't matter. It's not who I am, or who I'm ever willing to be. And they certainly won't be searching for me under that name."

"Please," was all he said.

"Sharon Stanley."

"Claire," Jacob started, his tone careful. "Why are they looking so hard for you? After five years of your not going to the authorities, I would think they would just stop bothering. Do you have something on them so dangerous that they won't stop trying to kill you?"

"They aren't trying to kill me. They're trying to take me back, which works to my advantage. I mean, they could have shot me a few times by now, but getting me into a vehicle is a lot harder."

Jacob quirked an eyebrow at her. "Is it just an ego thing? Returning the one who got away, back to the fold?"

She shifted on the couch then stilled, annoyed she'd done something to give away her unease. "Yeah, basically. They want to use me." She stood up. "Look, I've told you who to watch out for. Please, please be careful if you try to look into them. If they come to the office looking for me, just tell them I quit without notice. As long as you aren't acting all tough with them, they probably won't think twice about it."

"Damn it, Claire!" Ryan straightened away from the desk but didn't move closer to her. "Why won't you let us help you? This running obviously isn't working out so well for you. You can't live your life like this. One of these days you're going to slip and they *will* catch you, then what?"

Somehow the angrier he got, the calmer she became. "Then I make sure they have to kill me or die themselves. They won't get me back there."

He threw his hands up in the air. "So, you're basically on an extended suicide run. That's a great plan. Why bother living a life now if you're just going to be handing it over anyway? Excellent point."

Okay, not-so-calm now. She was annoyed to feel her throat closing in and that prickling sensation at the back of her eyes. "What the hell do you want me to do, Ryan? I *will not* go back. *Cannot* go back. I won't just sit here waiting for them to get me. So I run. That's the only option I have left."

"We're giving you another option. We can help you, if you would just trust us."

"Do you think you're the first people to say that? Well, you're not. Would you like to know what happened to the others who've tried to help me? Go ahead, guess!"

Jacob stepped up to where they were glaring at each other but they ignored him.

"It doesn't matter about others, we can—"

"Dead, Ryan, they're all dead! Do you really think I want any more deaths on my conscience? How callous do you think I am that I would let the death toll just keep rising while other people try to solve my problem? If you think I'm that much of a shit, than you should be glad to see the back of me. I'm leaving!"

She spun on her heel, nearly tripping over Jacob. Blinking hard to keep the tears back, she grabbed her purse and almost made it to the door before Jacob spoke.

"Tell me one thing, please, Claire."

Anger carried her the rest of the way to the door but she stopped with her hand on the knob, waiting. Why did she find it so hard to leave these guys?

"How do you think they keep finding you? You seem too smart to continually fall into old habits or contact people from your old life. How is it that they keep finding you after only a few months in each new life?"

Despair was creeping up, edging out the anger. She'd asked herself the same question so many times and had never come up with an answer. Each new life she tried harder, and yet they always seemed to find her eventually. She laid her forehead against the door, her shoulders sagging under the weight of her future.

"I don't know." How they even heard her answer she wasn't sure, it had come out so quietly. But they came to her, one on either side, and each put a hand on her shoulder. It shouldn't help, but somehow it made the burden a little bit easier. "They're just, always there. And there's always the strong chance that someone will die after I leave. But I have to go somewhere. I have to start over somewhere, live somewhere, work somewhere. How do I decide? How can I choose whose lives to put in danger next?" Tears escaped and she didn't have the energy to try to stop them.

"Honey," Ryan soothed. "You can't keep doing this to yourself. You have to let us help you."

"Don't you think I would if I thought it would work? But it won't and I've already put you at risk. Please don't make it worse. I don't know if I'll be able to keep going if I hear that you've been killed—that I've gotten someone else killed."

Ryan pulled her away from the door and into his arms. She let the embrace comfort her but used the fear of what could happen to them banish the tears. Pulling back her head, she looked up at him. "I won't risk it. I can't."

"Come sit down. I think Jacob may have figured out how they keep finding you." He led her back to the couch and sat with her.

Jacob resumed his seat in the chair next to her and leaned close, his elbows on his knees, his expression grave.

"I think it's possible they're using a psychic to track you. It would explain how they get close but not too close. There aren't many psychics good enough to pinpoint your exact location, especially from a distance."

She blinked at him, a new knot forming in her gut. He looked serious but... She rolled her eyes at him and glanced around for her purse, spotting it on the floor by the door.

"Claire," Jacob said, his urgent tone drawing her attention back to him. "I'm very serious. If they're using a psychic to track you, we might be able to help you disguise your spirit enough to keep you free. You can set up a new life somewhere, a permanent one."

Ryan tensed beside her but she had other things to worry about. Like the sweat breaking out on her brow and the knot in her stomach that was growing to the size of a football.

"I don't believe in psychics."

"Why not?" Jacob asked reasonably.

"I just don't. Not in psychics or witches or werewolves."

"No? What about Faeries?" Ryan asked, laughter in his voice.

"No, none of those things."

"Why?"

She rolled her eyes at Jacob. He was beginning to sound like a six-year-old.

"Because they don't exist! Besides, do you know how dangerous that would be? If there were psychics, like you said, they would know where I was going and be there waiting for me. The family would know who was trying to stop them and just kill them. They would know—" She broke off. This whole conversation was ridiculous.

"That's not the way it works, Claire. And you know it." Jacob's voice was calm, his face showing nothing but sympathy.

She reared back as if she'd been slapped. A sharp pain spiked behind her eye. "What the hell is that supposed to mean?" Instead of the indignation she was going for, she sounded terrified.

"I think you're psychic. I think you've blocked that part of yourself away so thoroughly that you've forgotten about it."

"Wh— I don't..." She couldn't seem to get a coherent thought together in her head, let alone out of her mouth. Pressing the heels of her hands to her eyes, she shook her head. "This is ridiculous, it's stupid. I'm not psychic."

"Honey, you have an enormous psychic shield around your mind. I've never seen anything like it," Ryan told her, as if that made everything clear.

Her hands dropped and her head snapped up. "Are you saying that *you* are psychic?"

"Well, no, not really." He smiled at her. Actually smiled at her, as if this wasn't the nuttiest conversation ever. "But I can usually recognize a psychic when I find one. They're pretty rare, though."

Her old friend anger was making a comeback and it felt good, so much better than the fear and despair. "That doesn't make any sense." She would have said more but Jacob reached out a hand to stop her.

"Claire, explain to me why you had to run and why they're trying so hard to get you back. You've said they were bad, but it's more than that, isn't it?"

"Why does it have to be more than that? You think I wanted to stick around with people who are willing to kill for their own gain? People who enjoy hurting others, and will use their own kids to do so? Do you really—"

"How did they use you, honey?" Ryan interrupted, his hand going to her back, smoothing up and down as if that tiny bit of comfort could make up for the hurt that they were wringing from her.

"What does it matter? They used me to hurt people. I was too young to understand, too stupid to hide the truth, and people died. My father died!" A sob burst from her throat, shocking her before she realized the words had escaped her mouth. Her head went light and dizzy. "I-I didn't mean that. I don't know why I said that." She rubbed at her temple, the headache from the day before back full force. It felt as if something were trying to burst through her head at the same time that something else was pounding on the outside, trying to get in. How long could her skull take the pressure?

"Are you okay?" Ryan moved his hand up to massage the back of her neck.

"I don't feel so great. That headache is back."

He moved, pushing her forward so that he could sit behind her, cradling her between his thighs, and began massaging her shoulders.

"Claire, it's not healthy for you to keep this all in. Eventually you're going to crack."

"I don't know what you're talking about."

Jacob handed her a bottle of water and some Tylenol. She hadn't even seen him get up. It wasn't good that she was being so oblivious, but she couldn't quite remember why .

"Will you let us help you?" Jacob asked. "We can ease the way a bit, help you see the shields you've created. You don't want them to crack on their own and leave you vulnerable, so you need to see them, be aware of them. Hiding from yourself is not the answer."

Ryan stopped the massage long enough for her to take the pills, then resumed. She ignored Jacob. Logic seemed to have taken a vacation and arguing with them was getting her nothing. She'd just let the massage and the medicine work their magic until she could think again, then be on her way. Finally.

Slowly her shoulders dropped away from her ears and her neck loosened up. She let it fall forward, her eyes closed, drifting in a hazy fog with no memories, no thoughts, just the melting goodness of the massage. Jacob's voice faded in and out, but she paid it little attention. He took her hands in his, his thumb brushing a light pattern in rhythm with Ryan's.

"Can you see the wall, Claire? It's impressive. Amazing. I've never seen anything like it. You must have started building it young, which is good, natural. You have to develop a way to control the energies coming at you. But you went a step too far. You walled your abilities off from your consciousness, separating a natural part of yourself."

She felt a tickling along her forehead but couldn't be bothered to investigate. Or was it inside her forehead?

"Let us in, let us show you." Ryan's murmur in her ear accompanied a change in the massage. He ran his strong fingers along the column of her neck, tipping her chin back until her head rested against his shoulder, then focused his attentions on her throbbing temples.

"Do you see it, Claire?" Jacob's low voice barely penetrated the fog. "Do you see the wall the same way we do? Huge gray bricks, stacked so tightly they don't even need mortar?"

She saw the wall as he described it, craning her mental neck up to see the top, but it stretched on and on and she had no idea if there was an end to it. Jacob's voice, sounding so far away, must be on the other side of the wall. She reached a hand out to touch it, shivering at the cold stone. Looking down she saw that it had tiny cracks in the foundation. Fear swept through her and she dropped to her knees, grabbing at the mud now thick beneath her feet, filling in the cracks. She had to fill them in, couldn't let anything through. Jacob's voice dimmed.

"It's important to have a door or a window in your wall. Some way to let in what you want and to expel what you don't want. Otherwise there will be too much pressure on it and it will eventually collapse."

Frantic now, she scooped more and more mud but the cracks were expanding. Her head felt as if it were going to explode. "It's cracking, Jacob, it's going to fall down. Ryan!" Some distant part of her was aware of their hands on her, their soothing, massaging motions continuing without pause. But she needed them inside, needed their help, and they were on the wrong side of the wall. "Help me, please."

"You just have to let us in, Claire. A little window. Tiny. Put it up high, so it's away from the foundation. You can do it."

She was afraid to stop working on the cracks but glanced up the endless expanse of wall. Could she make a window that would open and close only for her? She tried to imagine something, up high enough that it wouldn't affect the integrity of the wall, but low enough that she could see through, see what she was letting in. She imagined the thickest glass possible with a sturdy frame built deep into the stone. Immediately she could see the change. Afraid she'd screwed up, she shot to her feet, abandoning the cracks for the new threat. But the construction looked solid, no chance for anything to get through unless she opened the window.

And there, on the other side, stood Ryan and Jacob. They looked...different, somehow, but she wasn't sure. They smiled at her, proud and encouraging. Almost without her volition, her hand reached out and gave the window the slightest nudge to the right. A crack, only the smallest bit, and darkness overcame her.

CHAPTER FOUR

Claire collapsed into Ryan, her body twitching against his. He drew her physical form close while he and Jacob concentrated on what was happening inside her mind. His heart had swelled with pride when the small window had suddenly appeared in the imposing stone wall. The face on the other side had been frantic with fear but also flashed a spark of hope at seeing them. She'd reached out a hand and opened the window less than an inch. His heart had nearly stopped as her face went white and she dropped from view. But they were in, so now they could help.

Ryan concentrated on healing her, easing her headache while Jacob closed the window and added a touch of magic to the foundation of her wall. If it collapsed, she'd likely have a complete mental breakdown. He was amazed she'd lasted this long without ill effects. Denying such an intrinsic part of herself, literally walling it away within her mind, was shockingly unhealthy to the human mind.

"Claire," he murmured, stroking her hair, caressing her face. "Wake up now. I need to see your beautiful eyes."

Those eyes squinched up but remained closed. Since they did, he let a smile loose. Damn, she was stubborn. He really shouldn't find that appealing.

When the headache was completely gone he withdrew. The last thing he wanted to do now was piss her off for being where he shouldn't be, without invitation. It took Jacob another minute but then he, too, was fully removed from her mind.

Ryan leaned back against the couch, content to hold her in his arms while she recovered from her ordeal. As long as he didn't let his mind wander to her past, to what had caused her to build such an incredible barrier. A shiver racked her body and he squeezed tight. How had he not realized how small she was? How fragile?

Meeting Jacob's eyes, he opened their mental connection.

Did we fuck up? He let his doubts show, his fear for Claire.

No. The cracks were already there. If she doesn't face this, it will collapse around her and she probably won't recover.

Ryan nodded then rested his cheek against her hair. She'd managed to burrow her way into his heart, all while being abrasive and trying to run. Maybe he was a masochist. Whatever, it seemed to be working for him so he wasn't going to fight it. No, he was going to fight to keep it, her.

Her lashes fluttered and he adjusted her a bit more to his side so that he could see her face. In the span of a second it flashed from sleepy to furious. *Uh oh.*

She sat up straight but he did too so that he could keep holding her.

"That was *not* fun." She glared at Jacob then Ryan. He worked hard not to smile

because he didn't want to piss her off more, but she was so damn adorable.

"No," Jacob agreed, "I don't imagine it was. But I'm afraid it was necessary."

She faced him again. "Oh, well, gee, if you say so then I guess it's okay."

Jacob sighed. "Claire, you saw the cracks in your wall. That is not the sign of a healthy defense mechanism, let alone a healthy mind."

"Are you calling me sick in the head?" she demanded.

Throwing his hands up in the air, Jacob appeared to have

reached his limit with her. He stood up and stalked to the door without saying another word.

That seemed to take the starch out of her and she slumped back down against Ryan. He tightened his arms around her and she didn't complain. He couldn't decide if that was a good thing or not. As crazy as it sounded, he liked her stubbornness. Maybe it was because he was a warrior to his people, but most of the women he dated were so sweet and easygoing. He'd never thought it was a bad thing before, but now...now it just seemed so bland and boring. One thing about Claire, she wasn't boring.

"You feeling okay, honey? I think we were able to fix the headache this time." He knew it was a mistake the second the words were out of his mouth. She confirmed it by turning her head to glare at him.

"Excuse me?"

"Ah. Well. Yesterday, when you got your headache, we tried to cure it. But your shields were way too good, we couldn't get in far enough to heal your pain." She'd stiffened in his arms but he hurried on. "That's how we knew you were probably psychic. That shield was not normal for a human." Damn. His brain just didn't seem to know how to censor himself around her.

"I see. Would you happen to know how I got the headache in the first place?"

He definitely had a problem if he preferred her anger to this cold calmness.

"Well, that was sort of our fault. We thought you were a thief or spy, so we tried to read your mind to find out what you were doing at Teck Securities. We couldn't get in though, and it started to hurt you, so we tried a bit harder so that we could ease your pain."

She stood up and he immediately missed her warmth.

"So you invaded my mind."

He cleared his throat. "Well, you could say that. Or you could say that you repelled our advance, which was mighty impressive."

She rubbed her hands over her eyes before turning back to face him. "You're psychic." Somehow it sounded a bit dirty when she said it.

"Actually, no." *Jacob*, he thought, quickly filling his partner in on the situation, *you want to come help me out with this?*

No, I think I'll leave this one to you. You seem to be doing so well, so far.

He sent a mental glare through their connection and returned his attention to Claire. She was watching him with narrowed eyes and he wondered if she'd sensed their communication. Now that she was a tiny bit more open, psychically, there was no telling what she would be receiving.

"No," he continued, "we're not psychic. We're Fae."

She stared at him, her face going to that curious blankness that irritated him so much. Then she blinked and he felt better. No words seemed to be forming, but she didn't turn away, either, so he walked closer.

"Yes, we're from Faerie. We're here, in the human realm, as protectors. There are some Fae who think it's fun to use humans. Plus, the occasional demon who gets a little out of control. We stop them, send them back to be judged by their own, unless they've been seriously out of control—harming humans. Then we send back their bodies."

More blinking. Finally she opened her mouth, paused a moment, then spoke. "You and Jacob."

"That's right."

"I see. Are there a lot of Faeries and demons running around, then?"

"Not so many, no."

"And there are psychics too."

He nodded, refraining from pointing out that she was one herself.

"Witches, werewolves, vampires?" she asked.

"And more."

"Ah."

"Claire, none of this changes anything. These things were already out there, you just didn't happen to know about them."

"Right. Okay, well, I think it's about time for me to go."

He sighed. "Claire. You have to face this, deal with this. It's not about Jacob or me, so it's not just going to go away when you're not around us."

"It wasn't a problem until you tried to invade my mind. I think it'll be just fine once I'm gone."

"It wasn't, Claire. It couldn't have been. Tell me you weren't running down, getting headaches, stomach problems, something. Go ahead, tell me."

"What, you don't think it's normal to have migraines or ulcers when you're on the run from your homicidal family?"

"Maybe for a normal human, but for a psychic, for you, it means you've been denying too big of a part of yourself for too long."

"I never said I was psychic."

"Claire..."

She shot him one last glare, then turned and dropped onto the couch again. Encouraged, he sat down close to her. When she didn't move away, he took it as a good sign and put an arm around her shoulders. She snuggled in close, and just like that, his heart cracked open.

"Faeries," she muttered, half statement, half question.

"Fae. Yes."

"Named Ryan?"

"Well, actually it's pronounced with a long E. *Rían*. I only hear that at home, though, or occasionally Jacob will call me that when we speak telepathically."

"Right, telepathically. Where is he, anyway?"

"He wasn't real impressed with the way I was handling things. I think he figured if he made himself scarce you might be willing to come ask him questions when you were done pummeling me."

"So he wasn't the one invading my mind, back in your office?"

"Actually, that was more him than me. He's better at that, being subtle and not causing pain." He grimaced. "Usually."

"Well, then I should be more mad with him than you, right?"

"I...will let you make up your own mind about who you're mad at." He waited a beat. "Are you really mad?"

It was her turn to sigh. "I don't know. I'm too confused right now."

"Fair enough."

"So, if you can talk telepathically, what is he doing?"

Ryan sent the mental question to his partner. Rather than answering with words, Jacob sent him a picture of the stove, where he had omelets enough for three cooking.

"He's making breakfast."

At the mention of food, Claire's stomach growled. He squeezed her shoulder then urged her up. "Come on, let's get some food into you. You can yell at us later."

"Wait. Tell him to say a secret word when we get there, so that I know you talked to him."

He passed the request along, as well as a brief description of Claire's surprisingly good mood. When they reached the kitchen, Jacob glanced up, looked Claire in the face and said, "A secret word," then went back to working the omelets.

"Hmph." She crossed her arms and glared at Jacob, which Ryan found amusing. She took a deep breath and her stomach rumbled again.

He began setting plates on the table and she moved to help him. They got everything set just as Jacob brought the food over. His body may not be making noise, but Ryan was starving. They ate in comfortable silence, though Claire occasionally darted looks their way. It was so hard for her to open up to them, he got that, tried not to take it personally. She'd never had anyone to rely on, anyone she could safely count on to help her. It would be ridiculous to take it personally that she didn't just trust him with that. Ridiculous. If he kept telling himself that, maybe it would eventually sink in.

"That was delicious, Jacob, thank you," Claire said.

Ryan nodded his agreement around his last bite, then pushed his plate away.

"So. Faeries." Her voice held no particular inflection, which he was beginning to realize was a sign of trouble.

"Fae. From Faerie," he corrected absently while studying her face.

"Hmm." She glanced back and forth between them, then lowered her eyes to the table. "I'm not psychic."

Jacob opened his mouth to respond but Claire kept talking.

"I think, umm..." She swallowed hard and wrapped her arms around her stomach.

Ryan reached a hand out. When she didn't react, he settled it on her shoulder, wishing they weren't at the table so he could hold her in his arms.

She gave a little shake of her head and took a deep breath.

"When I was little, I used to feel things. Things that weren't...mine. It made it easier to know when I should stay away from people, when they were angry, or sometimes when they were a certain kind of happy and excited. The kind that got other people hurt."

Screw the seating arrangements, he didn't think he could listen to this with her sounding so far away and alone. He stood and plucked her from her side of the table and strode back to the study. When they were back on the couch, Claire sat up, though she made no move to get off his lap. He wrapped one arm across her legs to rest on her hip and left the other on her back.

"You're an empath," he prompted when she didn't say anything.

A tiny tremor ran through her at his words and he hated that she'd become so afraid of who and what she was. No wonder she'd blocked it away so thoroughly.

"When you're that age it's hard to know that most of the people around you barely tolerate you. It doesn't matter what their outward actions are if you know what they're really feeling." She paused for a long moment. "My dad loved me."

Ryan's gut clenched at the hopelessness of that statement. He didn't need to be psychic to know that this wasn't going to be good.

"I didn't realize that I was different, that I could feel things I wasn't supposed to. I didn't know I should hide it until too late. They started using it, using me. If they had a meeting and wanted to know if someone was lying. That sort of thing."

"How old were you?" Jacob asked.

"I don't know. Seven or eight, I guess."

They waited, letting her go at her own pace. Another shudder had him pulling her closer to him but her spine was stiff.

"He shouldn't have said goodbye," she said, her voice thick. "Who, Claire?" Ryan asked, afraid that he already knew. "My father. He should have known better."

"But he came to say goodbye? Tell you that he was leaving?"

"He pretended it was just for the day, just his normal goodbye. But I could tell, he was so sad but determined. I knew he wasn't coming back." She burst up from his lap, nearly falling before gaining her feet. "Stupid, he was so stupid!"

Ryan rose and so did Jacob, both keeping out of her way, letting her tell it.

"I knew he wasn't coming back and I cried. I begged him not to leave me. He was the only one who gave a shit about me and he was leaving. I was a stupid kid and I didn't think. Didn't think!" She was shouting now, tears falling, pacing between them like a caged tiger. "They heard me. They took him. I killed him."

The last came as a whisper and she'd stopped moving. She looked at him, her eyes begging for absolution. Something he was ready and willing to grant.

He took her in his arms, ignoring her stiffness. "You did not kill him. They killed him. You did nothing wrong. Claire, you were a child! Faced with losing the only person who cared about you, of course you cried and asked him to stay."

She shook her head against his chest. "I knew not to react, knew to hide my feelings. I knew!"

"Bullshit," Jacob answered. "Do you think he would be happy to know that you were blaming yourself for his death? He would know who was to blame, he would know who killed him. What would he tell you, Claire? Who would he blame?"

She shuddered, her whole body shaking with pain, but she didn't answer.

"Who, Claire?" Ryan stroked his hands up her back, twined his fingers through her hair and gently pulled back until he could see her face. Forcing her to meet his eyes, he asked again, "Who?"

He watched her struggle against the answer. How was it easier to blame herself? To blame the child that she had been?

"Her." It came out a croak but she cleared her throat and tried again. "My mother."

Jacob came up, resting one hand on her neck, adding his reassurances. "Her fault, not yours. Don't take that away from your father."

She looked at him, her eyes haunted. Then she turned a bit green and bolted for the door. Luckily the bathroom was directly across the hall. Ryan followed her in and held her hair back while she emptied her stomach of the breakfast she'd just eaten. She didn't even notice when he conjured a glass of water for her to rinse her mouth out with. Didn't object when he led her back to the study, sat her on the couch next to him.

"You know," he said after a few minutes. "This is going to sound horrible, but I think you're lucky they didn't love you." She gave him that expressionless face and he hurried on. "If they'd loved you, wanted to spend time with you, they probably would have made sure you turned out like them. You would have wanted to please them. You might have become...them."

She closed her eyes and leaned back against the couch. The silence was about to kill him but then she gave a tiny nod. Relieved, he took her hand in his.

"Claire," Jacob said softly, waiting until she opened her eyes and looked at him to continue. "I know you've had bad experiences before, letting people help you. I understand why you would be afraid to do that again. But we *can* help. We *are* very difficult to kill."

"Because you're faeries."

"Fae," Ryan corrected.

"Right. So, you're what? Immortal?"

"Just very long-lived," Jacob answered.

"Well, how old are you?"

"I'm three hundred and six."

She turned to look at Ryan. "And you?"

He cleared his throat. Somehow he didn't think she was going to like it. "One hundred and fifteen."

"Oh. Wow. I slept with a man older than my great-great-great-grandfather. Or something."

Claire waited for the squick factor to hit but it didn't. "Well, I guess that's okay, since your maturity seems to be stuck at about twenty-five." She slid a glance his way to see his reaction. First he blinked, then he gaped, then he laughed at exactly the same time Jacob did.

He had a nice laugh. They both did, actually, almost musical.

She smiled to show she'd been kidding, but still, it was weird. Faeries. Or Fae. Whatever. Taking in a deep breath, she tried to focus on what that meant. Could it be true? Could they be the answer she'd been afraid to look for? Because as much as she hated to admit it, Ryan was right. She could only keep going as she had been for so long. "Extended suicide run" wasn't so far off. But what choice did she have? Until now, none. Hope was a scary thing, though.

"So, long-lived but you can still be killed. Actually, let's back up a minute. What's the difference between being Fae and being psychic? So far all I've seen you do is talk to each other. Or read each other's minds." She looked around the room for inspiration. "I'm afraid I'm going to want more proof than that. What else can you do?"

"Tell me an object. Anything. I'll bring it here," Ryan suggested.

Her brow furrowed in thought for only a second. "A rabbit. No! That's stupid, hang on." No way was she making this easy for them. "How about a..." Damn, she was stuck on rabbit. Pull another one... "Okay, how about a...vibrator."

Oh my God, had she just said that? Apparently, as Ryan gave a choked bark of laughter and held up his hand, holding a large, purple vibrator, otherwise known as a Rabbit. Of course he would know what it was. Jacob looked on curiously until Ryan turned it so that he could see the little rabbit sitting on the dildo, its ears ready to buzz someone into bliss.

He handed it to her and she took it, then smacked him in the chest with it. Laughing, he took it back and *poof*—it disappeared to wherever it had come from.

"Don't worry, I'll make sure it's available if we want it later," he told her in a sexy purr.

"Great, but if I have that, I don't need anything else." She cocked an eyebrow at him but he just laughed.

"Oh, honey, I think we can work something out that will satisfy us both."

She opened her mouth to respond but was interrupted by Jacob clearing his throat. Again. Damn, she bet the poor man wasn't used to being forgotten or ignored, but somehow when she got going with Ryan, she lost track of who else was in the room.

"Anyway..." she drew the word out. "You said you weren't immortal, just long-lived. But you also said you were hard to kill."

"That's right."

Ryan moved his hand so that it was resting against her nape. He'd been doing that kind of thing all morning. She should probably shrug it off but it was kind of nice. It was unusual for her to trust enough, get close enough, for casual touch. Could she risk trusting them...with their lives?

"So if you got shot, say, two or three times?"

"It wouldn't feel great, but unless all three shots were directly to the heart, as long as we got to a healer relatively quickly, it wouldn't kill us. Or unless they managed to shoot our heads off, that's sort of hard to come back from."

"I see." And she did see, or thought she did. They were thinking they could get shot or stabbed, no big deal. Only it was a big deal. Because if they survived that by taking out whoever was after them, Uncle John would just send more. And more. Unless she asked them to kill her mother, grandfather and uncle, there would always be more. And she wasn't asking anyone to become an assassin for her.

And how successful could they be at their own work if they ended up devoting their time to surviving all the attempts on their lives? Plus, it wouldn't take long for Uncle John to realize that while they may be less vulnerable, their company—their employees—weren't.

Her breath wooshed out of her as reality hit. If Uncle John realized there were beings in the world that could survive gunshots and knives, if he realized there were faeries and demons and whatever else, the Smiths would stop at nothing to figure out how to use that to their advantage. She would rather be dead than unleash her family on the world with that kind of firepower behind them.

Bracing herself, she stood. She wasn't going to try to leave in anger, or even fear. It was just...time to go. Time to let them return to their lives.

"Look. I appreciate what you're trying to do. Really. But it's not going to work. You aren't thinking this through all the way, and while I'm so thankful you're trying, the longer I stay here, the more danger you're going to be in."

Ryan stood and tried to interrupt but she put her hand on his arm, quieting him. "You're forgetting that it's not just about you two. You have a company full of employees trusting you to keep them safe. You may be in less danger than most, but they aren't." She reached up and gave him a kiss, ignoring his silent reproach. She gave Jacob a peck on the cheek, too, then turned and walked out the door. They followed her to the foyer.

"Where will you go?" Jacob asked.

"I'm not sure. I've got some possible identities, I just need to decide who I want to be next and where it makes the most sense to take them." She turned back and looked at them. "I meant what I said. Thank you for what you tried to do, it means a lot to me. And..." She bit her lip, took a deep breath. "Thank you for making me face what's inside me. Now that I know it's there, I'll see if I can open up to it a bit, make it work for me instead of hurting me. I—" She broke off. There wasn't really anything more to say.

"We can send you to where you need to go. Back to the office, or wherever you like," Jacob offered, his tone carefully free of censure.

She shivered. "Magic."

"Yes."

She glanced at Ryan who hadn't said a word, then looked back at Jacob. "How about the Sheraton Hotel, by the airport?"

Jacob nodded and got a faraway look in his eye. "There is a restroom with only one person in it right now. I'll put you in the empty stall."

"That would be great, thanks, Jacob. Umm, will it hurt?" She hated herself for asking, but couldn't quite keep the words in.

His face softened. "No, it won't hurt." He held up his hand and there was a necklace in his palm. "Will you take this with you? If you need one of us, just hold the pendant in your hand and say our names. We'll come find you."

She swallowed hard against her closing throat. It was a lovely necklace, a silver rose just barely unfurled. Accepting it, she opened the clasp and put it around her throat. It nestled against her skin as if it had always been there.

"Thank you." She gave Ryan one last glance but couldn't read anything on his face. And then she was nowhere. By the time the thought had a chance to race through her mind, she was back, standing in a stall, toilet behind her and the sound of flushing to her right. *Well. Okay then.* That was weird, but handy. It was time to move on. Finally.

She walked through the lobby and strode through the front door. The doorman assured her that a taxi would take only a minute to arrive. True to his word, she was in a cab and on her way almost immediately. She chose a shopping mall ten minutes away as her destination and the driver left her to her thoughts.

Once the taxi had dropped her off, she walked a couple of blocks to a bus stop. The twenty-minute wait made it hard to keep her thoughts away from what had occurred over the last twenty-four hours, but she managed it by focusing on what she needed to do next. Step-by-step, the routine she knew by heart but couldn't stop repeating for fear she might start thinking. Wondering. Regretting.

No, it was too important to focus on what came next. No point thinking about what was already past.

It was time to pick a new name, a new destination. Usually she enjoyed this step, because she was always, *always* tired of being who she'd been, for however long it had lasted. She'd been Claire Fiordalisi for six months now, there was no reason she should be feeling so hesitant to give her up. No reason she should be reluctant to become someone else, to live the life meant for Joan or Erin or Samantha.

The bus arrived and she was glad to put aside disturbing thoughts and focus on where she needed to go. A transfer and a two-block walk got her to her destination around lunchtime. Perfect. It meant there was more traffic going into the bank, more people to mingle with. Still, she had her bank deposit box cleaned out, some of the cash converted into a cashier's check and was back on the sidewalk within forty-five minutes.

She'd picked the bank because it was within walking distance of a used-car lot. Buying the used car was an annoying process, as always, but she managed to drive off in a five-year-old compact. First she drove east, stopping at a post office on that side of town. Since she wasn't being actively chased, there was no reason to leave behind her second cache of goodies. Back on the freeway, she went north. Time to decide if she should keep north or head east once she hit northern Orange County. Maybe go to Nevada or Arizona. Even visit the Grand Canyon. But driving through miles of empty freeways across the desert wasn't quite what she wanted right now. Surprisingly enough, she wanted people.

The traffic was already heavy, which made the driving mindless. She couldn't hold off her thoughts any longer. Psychic. Well, empathic. That wasn't so bad, really, but it meant that there *could be* psychics, and that was not good. But Jacob had said that it wasn't as easy as their knowing where to wait for her. Still, the idea that they could find her just by thinking about it made acid rise up her throat. She breathed hard and swallowed.

How many times would she have died if the people who hated

her had been able to see what was in her mind? Worse, how many people's deaths would she have caused if her mother or grandfather had known what she had known? Learning to control her reactions and expressions had been hard enough. Control her thoughts too? Impossible. She probably would have just killed herself and been done with it. Horror at the very idea of how much damage she could have caused rolled through her and she turned on the radio, loud, trying to distract herself.

Too late, damn it, too late. Memories of the hurt she'd caused, of the deaths she'd been instrumental in, had her pulling over to the side of the road. *Don't be sick, don't be sick.* When had she gotten so fucking weak? She allowed a deep breath and a shake of her head before forcing herself back into the traffic. There was no use in thinking about the past. There was no reason to freak out about people being able to read her mind. The guys had told her there weren't a lot of psychics—or Fae, or demons, or whatever— running around town. They had to be right or she would've been in trouble a long time ago. Besides, *they hadn't been able to do it*, hadn't been able to read her mind.

Shaking her head to force herself on a new track, she decided to choose her next name. There were three possible IDs in her bag. Tara Small, Frances Huntington and Sloane Leddy. Maybe she could take Tara to San Francisco. Or Frannie to Colorado.

It was late and she hadn't eaten since breakfast, which she'd then tossed up. The sign ahead read Venice Boulevard. Her body made the automatic motions to exit the freeway without conscious thought. Spending time alone with herself in the car hadn't exactly relaxed her. She needed people. Crowds, energy to remind herself what real life was like, normal life with people whose biggest worry was what outfit to wear to the beach or what to eat for dinner. She'd never been to this part of Los Angeles, never been to the famous Venice Beach. Weren't the inhabitants supposed to be free-spirited and kooky? Maybe that's what she needed right now. She'd feel normal and sane by comparison.

She found herself on Washington Boulevard, passing small

motels and trendy sushi bars. The road ahead dead-ended at a parking lot. A car pulling out of a space on the street caught her attention and she pulled into the spot. Turning the engine off she sat, taking a look around. In front of her was a restaurant, people spilling out of the doors, music drifting easily on the night air. In her rearview mirror she could see a line of people outside a bar, waiting to be admitted. The thudding bass competed with the sweeter sounds from the place in front of her.

With a resolution that was more practiced than felt, she exited the car. Two police officers strolled by, chatting with a woman walking a dog. A teenager on a bike rolled past. She couldn't just stand here, damn it. Turning toward the sand, she headed for where she expected the boardwalk to be. Nothing. Okay, so maybe she hadn't quite gotten the right spot. Turning back, she examined the people, the restaurants, the bars. None of it appealed. Determined, she walked forward, skirting kids and dogs, trying not to let the dueling beats irritate her. Here were the crowds she was looking for, the energy she'd wanted. And it was so not working.

An ice-cream parlor appeared on the right and she entered it, relieved to be away from the happy throngs. There was only one couple inside, paying for their treats. She scanned the selections and ordered a small cup of chocolate chip. Part of her wanted to order a sundae, but it wouldn't have come close to last night's experience so she didn't try to compete.

While she waited for her scoop, she played with the necklace, then jerked her hand away when she realized what she was doing. Ignoring the curious look of the server, she took her ice cream and left the shop. She gave up on the idea of joining in with the natives and walked past her car to the parking lot. A pier extended over the water and she could only make out a few people walking its length. Summer hadn't quite arrived and there was a chill to the night air that seemed to be keeping most people to the restaurants and bars and off the sand.

A spoonful of creamy goodness had her finally relaxing, infinitesimally. Before Jacob's house, when was the last time she'd allowed herself such a treat? The answer was simple. Too long. Being on the run, constantly choosing to do things she didn't like or not to do the things she loved to make it harder for them to find her had taken its toll. She'd admit that now, if only to herself. Four years ago she never would have made the mistakes she'd made since hitting California.

Her pace was slow so it took a minute to walk far enough to be out over the water. She continued on, shrugging off a moment of unease when the light above her flickered and went out. The damn things did it all the time, it didn't mean anything. Shivering slightly, she angled to the right so her hair would blow behind her rather than into her ice cream. The wood railing was wide and dotted with holes for fishing poles. She leaned against it and watched the waves below.

There was something mesmerizing and calming about watching the ocean wash up to the land. If she ignored the lights from farther north, focused west into the inky darkness, she felt as if she were on the edge of the world, rather than just her continent. The ice cream and the damp night air were more than the shirt Ryan had picked out for her was meant to handle but she was determined to enjoy the moment. She allowed a snort of derision since no one was close enough to hear. She was a stubborn bitch, even against the elements. Smiling, she took another bite, then nearly choked as the meaning behind the Tinkerbell design finally sank in.

Her amusement faded quickly. Here she was, on Venice Beach, possible home of the kooks, though she was the only one around. Well, maybe the perfectly normal- looking people she'd already passed were crazy too. She didn't think she looked crazy, and yet...

Psychic. Empath. *Fuck.* She took another bite of ice cream, ignoring the shudders that were starting to work their way through her body. Cold, she was just cold standing in the brisk wind over the Pacific Ocean eating ice cream. Of course she was cold.

Ryan stepped up next to her. She didn't even flinch. Had part of her known he was there? At no point in her drive north had she felt as if she were getting away from him. Losing the connection she had with him. And when had that happened? She'd tried to convince herself she was being stupid. That she didn't feel any differently because there was nothing to feel. She took another bite as he leaned against the rail next to her, careful not to touch, probably waiting to see if she was going to try to pitch him into the ocean.

"Can I buy you some dinner to go with that dessert?"

CHAPTER FIVE

"What?" Thinking too hard, she hadn't been listening.

"Dinner. Can I take you out to dinner, since you've already got dessert?" As he said it he stepped behind her and ran his hands up and down her arms. "You haven't eaten since breakfast."

The warmth from his hands was almost intoxicating. And dangerous, she was sure, though it was hard to remember why. "You've been following me." It should upset her. It did, sort of. But not really in the way that it ought to. "You said you would let me leave." As soon as she said the words, she knew his answer.

"I did. You did. And besides, it was Jacob who said it."

She just nodded her head, took another bite.

"I'd like to take you out. On a date."

"You're crazy." The spoon scraped across the bottom of the cup as she chased the last of the ice cream.

"Maybe. Doesn't mean I don't want to go on a date with you."

That surprised a little laugh out of her. She tossed the empty cup and spoon into a trash can and turned to him. The wind whipped her hair over her sticky lips and she licked them clean. He held out a sweater for her, one that he hadn't been holding a minute ago.

"Thanks." This whole magic thing was crazy, but she couldn't deny that it was kind of handy too. She shrugged it on and just looked at him.

Too handsome for his own good, she judged. Those green eyes that must invite every woman to drown in them. And she seriously doubted she was the only woman who dreamed about having those strong arms wrapped securely around her. To say nothing of the strong face that radiated confidence. But mostly, she had to acknowledge that it was his complete attention and focus on her that she found so incredibly attractive. And slightly aggravating.

Had life been easy for him? It was tempting to think so, to dismiss him as incapable of understanding her. But he'd lived for over a hundred years. Chances were high that some of it had sucked. Of course she wouldn't know, because she'd made no effort to get to know him. Hadn't wanted to. It would be stupid to start now, to let him in further than he'd already burrowed.

"Okay."

He didn't give her a chance to change her mind, just took her hand in his and started walking back toward the street.

"My parents rarely come to this plane." He spoke assuredly, as if what he said was the most normal thing in the world. As if he'd known she'd been wondering about him. It gave her a start but she suddenly realized that she could examine her wall, her mental shield, and know that he wasn't inside. He was there, a slight presence, outside, waiting for an invitation.

"But when I was younger, they made the effort more often so that I would have a better sense of it. They wanted me to be able to come and go as I pleased, wanted me to feel comfortable when I was here. They had a house on the Galway Bay, in Western Ireland. To me, and to them I guess, now that I think about it, it was the best connection between the worlds. Watching the water of the bay, the waves lapping, the way the moon and the sun kissed the sea, all of it was so similar, no matter which realm we were in."

The light from the pier hit the waves as they raced each other to shore, as if they were running to something precious. She jerked her gaze away at the thought and looked forward. "Is that why you came to San Diego?"

"Partly. That and the sun, which is more common here than Ireland, I must admit. Plus, the demons are rather fond of Los Angeles, so it's a convenient waiting point."

"Demons. Are they...I don't know, like the movies?"

"Somewhat and mostly not. Just like everything else you mentioned—witches, vampires."

"Fae."

"Right. Sometimes the stories are close, sometimes they're worlds apart. Sometimes we encourage the latter, like misdirection."

She nodded in understanding. "Like with crime families." He cocked his head. "I guess so. Interesting."

"Are they always evil? Demons?" she asked.

"Not always, no. There are some who like it here better than Hell. They live their lives, mind their own business and we leave them alone. The problem is that the ones who are here because they don't have enough power in their own world, have powers that humans don't have much chance of withstanding. Which is why Jacob and I are here."

They reached the street and stopped, examining the restaurants close by. Without even asking each other, they headed for the quiet one with no line. Inside, they found a small space dotted liberally with tables. A waiter approached and Ryan pointed to an unoccupied corner. They took seats and Claire was ridiculously charmed that the table was scattered with nuts. They ordered drinks while she picked up an almond and the nutcracker and quickly shelled the meat.

"Why don't you have pointed ears?" she asked after the waiter left, before popping the almond into her mouth.

He smiled. "There are different sorts of Fae and a few of them have pointed ears, though not many. I will admit to looking slightly differently here than when at home. It's more of an aura, though, than looks. We use glamour when here to tone it down, blend in better."

She thought back to how he'd looked in her mind, through her window. "But you don't actually *look* different."

"No." He reached out and took her hand in his, waiting for more questions.

With her free hand she drew a swirly pattern on the tablecloth. "A hundred years is a long time. Do you mature like us?" She flushed, remembering her teasing from earlier, but he just rolled his eyes at her. "I mean, do you reach majority at eighteen?"

"Twenty, but close enough."

"It seems awfully young when you have so much more time."

He shrugged. "We tend to be in a hurry to gain our independence, even though most families are very close."

The waiter brought their drinks. Claire hadn't really looked at the menu but she didn't want to wait any longer. She checked the pasta listings and ordered the shrimp scampi. Ryan ordered the Jamaican sole and they watched each other until the waiter left.

"Have you ever been in love?" she asked, not sure where the question had come from or why she wanted to know. Or *if* she wanted to know.

His eyes dropped to the table and she would swear that a flush was creeping up his neck, though the light wasn't strong enough to be positive. He shifted in his seat and licked his lips before looking up and making eye contact again. She squeezed his hand.

"I thought I was. When I was fifty."

"You don't have to tell me if you don't want to."

"It's not a big deal. I just...I guess I thought I was ready for forever but she wasn't. And when it was over I couldn't understand how my feelings could change from being so certain to being...disappointed. I mean, if I'd been so in love, I should have been devastated. But forever is a long time for the Fae, and it turned out, once she said the things she did, I was just relieved not to have committed to forever."

She thought about that while the waiter dropped off their drinks. She had never allowed herself alcohol while out with a man, unwilling to risk the softening of her defenses, even slightly.

"So, what? There's no divorce in Faerie?"

"It's not that, exactly, though it's very rare. But there's magic to joining your life with someone in Faerie. It's not just words, a signature, a small ceremony and a party, like it is here. Well, it is those things, but more. Speaking a promise, saying those words with intent, to the Fae, calls forth our magic. It's...binding."

Not really sure she understood but uncertain she wanted to know more, Claire took a sip of her drink. It was well-flavored but strong and she felt the small path of warmth all the way down to her stomach. It was similar to the warmth she felt from his hand on hers, radiating up her arm. She liked it, had liked it even more when his hands had been all over her body. She wanted that again, wanted more.

Scooting her chair in closer to the table, she eased her left leg out until it touched his. She wished they weren't both wearing jeans. Glancing up, she met Ryan's eyes. He must have seen something in hers, some change, because she was able to watch the heat flare in his. The intent look of sharing washed away, replaced by lust and admiration. He broke the stare, his gaze flicking around them, double checking their surroundings. When he came back to watch her, the tiniest of smirks nudged his lips up.

With no more warning than that, her jeans disappeared. As did his. She blinked at the feeling of his heavy calf against hers and wiggled her butt to see what she was wearing now. Shorts. Jean shorts that were awfully...short. The laughter bubbled up out of her even though she tried to keep it down. It was just so crazy. Here she was with a man more than a hundred years old, a man who could use magic, and he'd given her Daisy Dukes so that they could play footsie—or was that legsie?—under the table of the nice restaurant he'd had to chase her down to bring her to. Her world was definitely changing, and for once, it seemed to be for the better.

He smiled at her laughter, then gave her a sheepish shrug when she let it trail off. It suddenly occurred to her to wonder what he'd given himself to wear. She kicked off the sandal that had replaced her tennis shoes and brought her toes to Ryan's leg. The waiter appeared with their food and she thanked him absently while keeping her attention on the man before her. She ran the side of her foot up his calf, pausing to play at his knee for a bit. Obligingly, he stretched his leg out toward her. She curled her foot around so that the toes led the way as the top of her foot ran along the underside of his thigh until she met fabric.

The way his breathing picked up pleased her. The fact that he shifted in his seat— presumably adjusting himself—but was careful not to dislodge her foot, pleased her even more.

"Careful, Claire," he murmured. "Don't start what you aren't willing to finish."

She moved her toes back and forth along his thigh, thinking. How far did she want to take this? Pretty much all the way. But not too fast. She wanted more talking and more food first. Wanted him to be as hot and bothered as she seemed to be making herself. Dropping her eyes to her plate, she stabbed a shrimp with a fork and brought it to her lips. She looked back at him and slowly eased the buttery morsel between her lips as she dragged her foot back down his leg until it once again rested on the floor.

His eyes narrowed and she resisted the urge to smile in triumph. That wasn't exactly the reaction he'd been hoping for, she knew. Keep him guessing, that was her new plan. Finally he picked up his own fork and began eating.

"So, what's it like there?" she asked. "In Faerie."

He looked thoughtful while he chewed then took a sip of his wine. "It's beautiful. You know when you see an amazing view here, or the light falls just so and you stop and look around because it's stunning? It's always like that there. Every part of it."

"Wow. Do you get jaded? So used to your surroundings that you forget to appreciate it?"

"No, because we're connected to it. The magic that keeps the land is the same magic that fills us. It's a part of us and we're a part of it. If we died, the land would decay. If the land was somehow corrupted, we would probably get sick and eventually die."

He cut off a bite of his fish and gestured with the fork in her direction. She nodded and opened her mouth, closing her eyes to savor the rich flavors of the sauce combined with the delicate fish. Delicious. Opening her eyes, she watched him watch her as she ran her tongue along her lips to clean up any sauce that had strayed. He retaliated by bringing his foot to her leg, much as she had done. He ran it slowly up her calf, under her knee and along her thigh, bringing his heel to rest on the chair between her legs. His foot just barely touched the inside seam of her shorts and she had to force herself not to press into his promised heat.

"How long have you been set up here? And how often do you go home?" she asked. She needed to distract him a bit and she was curious about how much of this world he considered home. Maybe it was just a job and he went back to Faerie every weekend.

He pressed his toes in just a bit. Enough that she could feel contact but not any real pressure. She felt herself getting wetter and fought hard to keep from squirming into him. Instead she drank from her glass then carefully cleaned her lips with her tongue. His eyes followed the action and she cleared her throat. He glanced up in question and she cocked her eyebrow at him.

The flush was small, just a bare gracing of red on his face, but it was enough for her to call this round a victory. Of course, his foot still rested on her chair and she was still fighting not to ease into the pleasure that he offered.

"Well, Jacob has been here for over a hundred years. He invited me to train with him about forty years ago, so at that time I came and went frequently. When he asked me to become partners with him about ten years ago, we set up this company in San Diego. I go back to Faerie at least once or twice a month to visit, but this is my home."

"For now."

He inclined his head. "For now and for the foreseeable future." The words were punctuated by a careful increase of pressure of his foot. Her clit pulsed and her hips canted forward of their own accord.

She twirled a forkful of pasta and brought it to her mouth,

careful to let long strands of pasta hang free. Then she sucked it up, slowly, until the last strand passed between her lips. While he was distracted, she brought her foot up his leg again and mirrored his position. It was a risk, because the movement settled his foot more firmly against her, but it also allowed her to reciprocate. She found his cock and rubbed up its length, curling her toes for the best contact. He actually let loose a small moan and she grinned. Until he began making little pulses with his own toes. Her fork clattered to the plate just as the waiter stopped by to ask if they needed anything.

"I'm done," she nearly shouted.

"Just the check," Ryan said at the same time.

He pulled his foot back and she waited a beat, pressed in just a bit, then pulled her leg down. Immediately she was back in her jeans and tennis shoes. She pushed her chair out and stood. He started to stand too, a look of panic on his face, which probably shouldn't have reassured her so much but it did.

"I'm going to use the restroom, I'll be right back."

He sat back down, watching her carefully.

She ignored him and walked toward a hallway, following a sign to the ladies' room. Inside, she sat on a bench and rested her head in her hands, the necklace swinging like a pendulum. Was she really ready to do this? To give him so much more of herself than she'd given any man...ever? It was probably stupid. It was probably dangerous. But she couldn't seem to help herself. Well, stupid or not, she was in. *In over your head.*

Walking back through the restaurant, she watched Ryan. He had such a presence, strong and confident. Sexy as hell. And the heat in his eyes as he tracked her just about melted her bones. Maybe he knew that, because he stood and offered his arm, leading her out of the restaurant.

They were silent, walking to her car. Once inside, she gripped the steering wheel. "I'm not sure where to go."

"I know a decent hotel in the area. Will you let me take you there?" he asked. His hesitance told her what a pain she'd been since he walked into her office. She was okay with that, but it made her wonder what it was that he saw in her that kept him on the chase.

She nodded her head, turned the key and followed his directions. When he indicated a driveway, she turned in, only realizing where they were when the valet stepped forward. Not bothering to look at Ryan, she asked, "The Ritz-Carlton?"

"What? It's decent and convenient." She could hear the smile in his voice and let it carry her out of the car, refusing to be embarrassed for the cheap thing while the valet handed her a ticket and gave her a smile and welcome.

They went inside and directly to the check-in counter. While Ryan spoke to the employee she rested her hand on his hip. When the woman began click-clacking away on her computer, Claire slid her hand around his front and down his hipbone. She didn't stray over to his cock, but let the possibility linger. His breath hitched. Resting her other arm on the high counter, she watched him work with the woman, not bothering to listen to the conversation. He was polite but distracted, shooting her looks the whole time. She traced his hipbone and made a mental note to explore the area with her tongue later.

Apparently finished with the business of checking in, Ryan grabbed her hand, spun and stalked toward the elevator, pulling her along behind him. They arrived just as the doors opened and two women stepped out into the lobby. A man remained inside and Ryan jabbed at a floor button. She guessed he'd been hoping they would have the elevator to themselves and gave him a coy look from underneath her eyelashes. At least, she hoped it was coy. She'd never attempted the maneuver, but it seemed to work. He stuck his hands in his front pockets and kept his eyes on the ground where he couldn't see her in the mirrored doors.

The car slid to a stop and the doors opened. The stranger got off and the second the doors were fully closed behind him Ryan moved toward her. She put a hand out to stop him, glancing upward. She didn't know if there were cameras up there, but until she knew otherwise, she was going to assume so. His jaw clenched tight and he went back to leaning against the wall, his hands resuming their place in his pockets. The move only served to draw attention to the bulge straining against his jeans but she decided against mentioning that to him.

This time when the elevator stopped and the doors opened, he grabbed her hand without even looking at her and nearly yanked her out and into the hallway. His much longer legs gave him a natural stride about a mile wider than hers so she was forced into a near jog to keep up. Oh, no, he was so not going to drag her down the hallway like a recalcitrant child. She gave an extra little burst of speed to catch up fully. He had just enough time to look back over his shoulder and give her a grin in response before her foot snagged his and he went flying. To his credit, he released her hand immediately rather than bring her down with him. He rolled over onto his back and stared up at her, an expression of pure disbelief on his face. She just cocked her eyebrow at him, careful not to smile.

He closed his eyes and breathed deeply. She got the distinct impression he might be counting to ten. Or twenty. Was he counting in English, or did they have their own language? Leaving him to it, she leaned against the wall and folded her arms against her chest. Eventually he sat up. She figured it was a sign of how much she liked him that she resisted the urge to ask him how high his count had gone and risk aggravating him further.

"Would you care to explain?" he asked, rising to his feet.

"You were dragging me down the hall like a puppy." She was having a hard time keeping the smile at bay and wasn't surprised when his gaze focused on her twitching lips.

"You could have asked me to slow down," he pointed out, leading the way farther down the hall before stopping in front of a door and sliding the key into the lock.

"Oh. Hmm, good point. I'll try that next time."

The little green light flickered on and she heard the click of the lock disengaging but Ryan was too busy banging his head against the door to open it. She reached around him and pushed the heavy door until he was forced to straighten up or fall through.

"What? You're right, I should have said something. I'm sorry. But that doesn't mean you weren't wrong too, pulling me down the hall like a caveman."

He stared at her for a full twenty seconds before he started to laugh, allowing her to release the smile she'd been holding back and join him. He pulled her to him.

"Ah, Claire, what am I going to do with you?"

"Ravish me?"

"Good idea, let's go with that."

He had her shirt off before he'd finished the sentence and was working on her jeans button while she toed off her shoes, clutching his arms for balance. They made for a wobbly pair but managed to do it all without falling. Soon she was wearing only her bra, panties and the pendant.

"Will you do me a favor?" she asked when he made to remove his own clothes.

He paused, waiting to hear more. Smart man, he was learning.

"Will you leave your jeans for last? I think that's so sexy, and I want a good mental image of it, not just my imagination."

"That I can do." He flashed her a grin and pulled his shirt off, then shucked his shoes and socks. She moved in to open the jeans. Letting her knuckles press into his tightly muscled stomach, she worked the button open and let her hands fall down, brushing his bulging package.

He drew in a gasp and she licked her lips, loving the play of muscles as his chest expanded and his stomach contracted. She took a step back and just looked. He was gorgeous, fucking gorgeous. The waistband of the jeans rode low, leaving the hipbones to jut out invitingly.

"Mmmm." She couldn't keep the small moan inside.

"I agree. You look delicious."

"Oh." She licked her lips. "That's a good idea. One of these days I'd like to get a bottle of chocolate syrup and make a sundae out of you."

He managed some sort of choked sound but she was too busy

landing on the bed where he'd thrown her to pay much attention. His lips descended on hers and she welcomed him. Her fingers found their way into his hair, sliding through the silky strands.

After a small eternity he released her mouth and looked at her. "You make me crazy."

The expression on his face was terrifyingly sweet and her heart lurched. She reached up to take his mouth with hers, pretending it wasn't an excuse to close her eyes and redirect her brain. The taste of him, the feel of him, hell, even the smell of him. All of it combined to make her damn near giddy. This time when he pulled back she made her move. Bringing her hands between them she shoved against his chest. He let her push him over until he was on his back.

She set her hands on his shoulders and leaned her weight into them, adjusting her seat, allowing her panties to slide against his crotch. The rough jeans gave her almost too much sensation before she settled down over his upper thighs. His hands came up to hold her hips but he made no attempt to move her, just let his thumbs brush along her thighs, curving his fingers around to her butt. Leaning down, she placed a kiss over his heart, then gave the spot a small bite. He tightened his fingers on her but he didn't move.

She moved lower and traced the hipbones that she'd lusted after earlier. She gave a long lick, then nibbled along the waistband of his jeans. He inhaled sharply and she followed the hollowing of his stomach with her tongue.

She sat up again and traced his pecs, circled his nipples.

"Claire," he growled, as if warning her.

"What?" Damn, that sounded too breathless. She inhaled deeply. It didn't hurt that the movement also refocused Ryan's attention on her breasts.

"Touch me."

It sounded an awful lot like a demand, but it was also a good idea. Not one to cut off her nose to spite her face, she decided to go with the suggestion. Yeah, suggestion, that sounded better.

She plucked his nipples with her fingers but her attention was on his abs. Oh yeah, the way they bunched and tensed in reaction to her fingers was amazing. He brought his hands up and around her back, sliding under her panties to cup her ass. She lowered her mouth to his stomach and licked a trail up to his chest, veering off at the last minute to pull hard on one of the nipples waiting for her.

"Mmm, that's good, honey."

He had better access to her butt now with her new angle. One finger slid over her asshole, then circled it. She squeaked and tried to pull away. His grip on her was firm though, so she bit his nipple in retaliation. He chuckled but moved on, so she relented and used her tongue to soothe. When he eased one finger through her wetness, she moaned against his skin but figured it was time to rethink her plan. She gave one last wet kiss to his sternum, sat up and reached behind her to unclasp her bra. He immediately moved his hands to help her remove the garment. Such a gentleman. He answered her grin with one of his own until she dropped the bra. His focus moved to her unbound breasts.

His hands came up to cup them almost reverently and she arched her back, urging him to do more. He squeezed the globes then pressed them together, licking his lips. She closed her eyes for a minute, enjoying the sensation, then opened them and focused on her next task. The jeans that had been so damn sexy before were now an irritating inconvenience. Grabbing the zipper, she would have pulled down but his hand on hers stopped her.

"Careful there!" He eased the metal prongs open while she tried not to laugh. Tried being the operative word. The glare he gave her wasn't even close to his best, so she didn't take it seriously. But she did lean down and kiss the flesh exposed by the now- open V of the pants. She curled her fingers around the top of the jeans and pulled down. Unsurprisingly, Ryan cooperated by lifting his hips into her lips. She smiled against his skin and pushed until the jeans were clear of his butt. He used his legs to shimmy them the rest of the way down and she resumed her seat on his upper thighs.

She leaned over, letting her belly brush his erection, and put her hands on his shoulders again. Pressing hard, she slid them down his chest, over his stomach, to either side of his cock reaching up toward her, until they rested on his thighs, just between her own. His breathing was hard, but so was hers, she realized. His eyes glittered with lust and she thought hers must too. He licked his lips and she couldn't help an answering swipe with her own tongue. Damn, he was almost too much. She shook her head and looked down at his cock. No need to play coy, she figured, and grasped it with both hands, one above the other.

"Oh, fuck, Claire."

"Tell me what you like, Ryan." She twisted her hands in opposite directions.

"Your mouth. Put your mouth on me." His hands came to rest on her knees, squeezing tightly.

"I don't know. You look kind of big for that. But my hands are a bit dry, I'll admit. Maybe we do need some lubrication here." She released her right hand and lifted off her heels enough to slide her fingers under the elastic of her panties. Finding plenty of cream, she coated her fingers and pulled them free. His mouth was open in shock as she brought her slickly coated fingers to his shaft and slowly lubed him up.

She squeezed then relaxed, twisted then pumped, never using the same motion more than a couple of times in a row until he was bucking beneath her. Then she lowered her mouth over the head and enveloped it in one quick move.

He tasted salty and musky and a little bit like her. He tasted addicting. She swirled her tongue, never letting the movement of her hands stop. Setting her teeth gently below the head, she sucked in as hard as she could. With a bellow, he erupted. She took what she could and let the rest dribble down to coat her fingers, now moving much more softly along his shaft.

"Claire," he whispered.

"Hmmm?"

"Come here."

She dropped a kiss on the head then looked up at him, licking her lips clean. He looked worn-out, but she couldn't be sorry, she'd enjoyed the hell out of that. A first for her.

Watching his heavy-lidded eyes, she crawled up the bed and dropped down at his side. She broke eye contact and rolled to her back, suddenly uncertain. He took her hands in his and brought them to his chest, laying hers over his rapidly beating heart.

"Am I still alive, then?" he asked.

"Feels like." She patted his chest, matching the internal rhythm.

"That's good to know."

"I thought you were hard to kill," she teased.

"Apparently I am. If that didn't do the trick, I don't know what will."

She laughed and turned into him, resting her head so that her ear was over his heart. How could she joke about his dying? Well, more about his living. Maybe it was time to remember that living was just as important as not dying. And something she hadn't been doing a lot of.

"Ryan?"

"Yeah."

"Do you really have some way of keeping me free from the psychics?" Was that her voice, sounding so small and tiny?

He squeezed his arm tight around her. "Yes."

She frowned. "But you don't think that's what I should do."

He sighed. "Claire, I'm past thinking I know what's best for you, or that your opinions on the situation aren't well thought out and valid. So if that's what you decide, I'll help you. I just...hate to see the bad guys get away with it. It's a thing with me, I guess."

"I'm not really thrilled with it myself. But..."

"I know. I understand." He dropped a kiss on her head. "I think I can move again."

"That's good to hear."

"How many times do you think I can make you come before you pass out?"

She blinked against his chest. "Umm. Is that a trick question?"

"More a statement of intent."

"Oh. Okay. So it's rhetorical? Because I've never come more than once in a night."

"Well, that's not much of a challenge. You barely have a record to break. Although, you do have a record for passing out—"

"Hey!" She sat up to get better leverage for hitting him but he used her momentum against her, lifting her up and dropping her back down so that she was once again on her back, this time with his heavy body looming over hers. He leaned down but instead of kissing her he winked and moved lower, one hand coming up to cup her breast while his mouth sucked in her nipple. She had sensitive nipples so it didn't take long to have her moaning. He paid attention though, responding to her movements, never taking her too far, never letting the pleasure edge over into pain.

He settled his leg between hers and she ground herself against it shamelessly. The sensation he was wringing from her breasts zinged straight down to her clit, which she worked against his knee. A gentle tug on one nipple while he sucked on the other, combined with a firm press between her legs, sent her over into a relatively gentle climax. She shuddered and sighed, then relaxed beneath him.

Ryan gave a last careful kiss to her now-supersensitive nipples and kissed his way between the valley, down to her bellybutton. She squirmed and grabbed his hair into her fist and he took the hint, bypassing the spot she didn't like anyone to touch with a quick kiss just below it. Releasing his hair so he could remove her panties, she didn't exactly relax when he kissed her pubic bone then breathed against her waiting, wet pussy.

Her insides clenched in anticipation as he breathed against her. "Ryan, please."

He licked her, from bottom to top. "Is that what you want, Claire?" "Yes, more."

Instead of licking her again, he eased two fingers into her. She squeezed his fingers as tightly as she could. He closed his lips around her clit and she cried out, clenching her thighs around his shoulders. He let loose a growl that vibrated into her, twisting his fingers inside her then twisting them around to find that spot that only she had ever found before him. She came, crying out his name, and yet the pressure wasn't really released. She needed more. Needed him inside her, and not just his damn fingers.

He busied himself with the condom then surged up her body, his chest rubbing against her sensitized breasts, wringing a moan from her as he swooped down for a kiss. She opened for him, wanting him, needing him, ready for him. He slipped inside as if he were born to be there and she could do nothing but welcome him home.

His hands came up and cradled her head, his thumbs tracing her cheekbones, threading his fingers through her hair. With a last sweet kiss he pulled back and looked at her, keeping eye contact as his cock slowly entered her. Her knees came up, squeezing his hips, urging him on. Refusing to be hurried, he glided all the way in. When he pulled back out, leaving only the tip inside her, she growled at him, but he just watched her, searching her face for...what? She arched her hips into him but he moved back. Bringing her arms around him and trying to pull him closer accomplished nothing. Letting the irritation show, she dropped her arms back to the bed and scowled.

"Can I fix your hair?"

Huh? "What?"

"Your hair. It's awful. I want to see what it really looks like. Let me fix it."

"Sometimes you're kind of an asshole."

"And?" He drove back into her, taking her breath away.

"And I don't fuck assholes," she said, once she could speak again.

"Who do you fuck?" he asked, raising both eyebrows.

She frowned. "That's the wrong expression. You're supposed to arch one eyebrow at a time for the maximum superiority affect."

His brows slammed down and together and he scowled.

"What?" she taunted. "No sexy quirk for you? Jacob does it rather well, I've noticed."

"I'm Fae, not Vulcan." He pressed his groin into hers.

She couldn't hold back a gasp but it didn't keep her from cocking her eyebrow at him. "Am I as sexy as Mr. Spock?" She managed to get the question out despite the fact he'd begun moving in and out of her again.

"You never answered my question."

She had to think harder than she should've to remember what the hell he was talking about. Oh, right, fucking assholes. "Doormats."

He stopped again, blinking at her. "You fuck doormats?"

She nodded, arching her hips up. "Generally, and not very often." She brought her nails down his back in a not-so-light scratch until she could grab his ass and urge him back into movement. Abandoning the conversation, he finally took her hint and began to move again, no longer showing the careful restraint of before. Instead of urging him on, her hands were now clinging to him for support. She blew into her orgasm with almost no warning, screaming into his shoulder as he lodged himself deep inside her and came.

He collapsed on top of her, but only let his weight rest on her for a minute before rolling over to his side. He pulled her with him so that they ended up both on their sides, facing each other. Giving into the crazy lightheartedness she'd only ever felt with him, she arched her eyebrow at him. She thought she caught a glimpse of a smile on his face before he pushed her back over and lowered his head to her neck, giving her a huge, wet, raspberry.

She convulsed into laughter, unable to fight him off as he held her down, moved lower, and vibrated another raspberry into her stomach.

CHAPTER SIX

Ryan woke up fast, his arm reaching across the empty expanse of bed. His heartbeat was so loud in his ears he almost didn't hear the toilet flushing in the bathroom. As soon as he realized what it was, he collapsed back onto the bed, releasing a gush of air. He rolled to his side, his back to the doorway so that he'd have a little more time to compose himself. He tracked the sounds as she used the sink, opened the door and padded across the plush carpet. The bed dipped behind him but he didn't move. When her small, warm hands slid over his shoulder and down along his chest, he rolled to his back, careful to keep the relief from showing on his face.

The room was dark but he could make out the sleepy look on her face. She made a soft little sound and curled into him, rested her head on his chest and went back to sleep. He'd sort of lost count of how many orgasms he'd dragged from her after their first bout, but she had every right to be exhausted, that was for sure. He plumped the pillow under his head and idly ran his fingers through her hair. Probably mentioning his distaste for it in the middle of sex had been rude, but he couldn't help himself. He wanted to know the real Claire, and the overdyed mess was a constant reminder that she was still pretending to be someone else. Hell, he still thought of her as

Claire, even though he knew it was a name she wasn't going to keep. It shouldn't bug him as much as it did, but names were important to the Fae. And she was important to him.

She shifted against him, bringing her leg up to hook over his, then settled back into sleep. He swirled a nonsensical pattern over her shoulder as he thought about his options. Unfortunately, he couldn't exactly force her to see things his way. How could he convince her that he and Jacob were perfectly capable of protecting her? But understanding her hesitation and concern wasn't the same as agreeing with her. He sighed and closed his eyes, because it did mean that he couldn't just bowl over her objections and act in spite of them. He respected her and that meant he had to respect her opinion of the situation.

The next time he woke up Claire was on her stomach, her face turned away from him. He traced a finger up the pale expanse of her back, enjoying the shiver that tracked his movements. She lifted her head, turned to face him and smiled. His heart melted, which probably should have hurt, but he was too full of euphoria to feel it. The answering smile he gave must have been a bit feral because her eyes went wide and she grinned. It was all he could do to grab a condom before attacking her. She tried to help and they fumbled the package until he pulled it away from her, ripped it open and sheathed himself.

They came together, lips to lips, chest to chest, legs wrapped around each other. He surged into her, his dick finding its way with no trouble, eager to return to the warmth that she offered. She erupted around him and he had to grit his teeth to keep from doing the same. He waited until her muscles had stopped quivering before he began moving again, sliding in and out, slow and easy, waiting until her nails scored his back and her cries soothed his heart before he abandoned easy and went with hot, hard and fast. He came in a rush, burying his face in her damn hair, smiling into her ear as she followed him over.

"Claire. Will you promise me something?" he asked, the fear of waking up not knowing where she was still hanging over him. He rolled to his side and propped his head up on one hand, the other resting lightly on the curve of her belly.

She tensed only slightly, which he took as a good sign. It was amazing how his perspectives had changed in a couple of days.

"What?"

"Promise me that if you're going to leave, you'll tell me? I've already promised not to stop you, so..."

"You didn't seem to have any trouble following me," she pointed out.

"Well, that was because I put a tiny spell on your shirt that day. But I can't rely on you not changing your clothes occasionally, and besides, I'd rather have your promise."

She stared up at the ceiling for a minute, then turned to look at him. "I promise, but the minute you try to stop me from leaving, the promise ends."

"Fair enough."

They shared a shower and if Claire remembered the last time they'd done so, she didn't let it show. He conjured them both clean clothes and he thought she'd had to resist a smile before pulling on the blue t-shirt with Tinkerbell sitting on the shoulder, legs dangling saucily close to the upper swell of Claire's breast.

He didn't ask where she was planning on going, just opened the door and followed her out, taking her hand in his as they made their way down the hall. Which reminded him of her move from the previous night. He'd been so eager to get her inside, to get inside her, that apparently he'd been dragging her down the hall, though he didn't quite remember it that way. Still, he couldn't help but smile at her method of slowing him down. At the time he hadn't exactly found it amusing, but now... Well, she was just so damn cute.

He'd called down to the valet stand so the car was waiting for them as they exited the hotel. While he handed the ticket and cash to the attendant who held the passenger door open for Claire, she walked around the front and slid behind the wheel. Well, he could hardly fault her, it was her car and she presumably knew where they were going. He was just glad she didn't peel away, leaving him standing there like a dumbass.

When he'd taken his seat and latched the belt, she eased out of the driveway and onto the small street. He had to actually bite his tongue to keep from asking where they were going. Out of long-standing habit he watched the side mirror, wishing he had access to the rearview, opening his other senses to compensate. He didn't spot anything out of the ordinary and remained quiet as she maneuvered the car onto the main road and headed north.

"So, Florida," he prompted. "I've never lived there. Blue water, Disney World, Cape Canaveral."

"There are lots of places with pretty water. I've never been to Disney World. I'll admit, watching a shuttle launch is pretty cool."

"You lived in Florida and never went to Disney World? Is that legal?"

She snorted. "I'm sure the same is true for plenty of Floridians. It's a big state. But seriously, I can't imagine any of my family going there, even to take a child they liked."

"Well, it's more fun as an adult than a child, anyway. Disneyland is just as good, in my humble opinion. And it's in California, which makes it better, actually."

"Sorry, haven't been there, either."

"That's just wrong. How long were you in San Diego? It's not that far."

"I didn't go to the Zoo or the Wild Animal Park, either."

"I say we fix it. You can turn around and we can go to Disneyland, or you can keep heading north and we'll go to Magic Mountain instead."

"I'm not twelve, Ryan. And I promise, I don't feel as if I've been missing out on some grand adventure, not having been to any amusement parks."

He might have let it go, except he didn't really believe that last part. Something in her voice made him think she had missed it, even if she couldn't acknowledge it to herself.

"I told you, it's much better as an adult than a twelve-year-old.

Besides, what else do you have planned for the day?" He reached over and took the hand she'd rested on her thigh. "Trust me."

They stopped at a red light and she turned to look at him. Finally she shrugged. "All right. But it will have to be Magic Mountain. I'm not turning around just to see mice."

He was pretty sure his smile was a bit ridiculous, but he couldn't help himself. "Good enough. So, Florida and San Diego. What was in between?"

"Let's see. Newark, Columbus, Wichita, Dallas, Colorado Springs. Smaller cities here and there. This past winter I was in Michigan." She gave an exaggerated shudder.

The drive was fast as they discussed the pros and cons of the many cities they'd lived in throughout the United States. He wasn't surprised that they'd never lived in the same place before now. Sometimes things weren't meant to be until they really were meant to be. He was saddened, though, at how rarely she'd been able to take advantage of what he considered the pros of any city. She'd existed in each place, but she hadn't really lived. As they started up the long driveway into the amusement park, he watched her eyes grow a little wide at the size of the roller coasters.

She paid the attendant at the parking kiosk, giving Ryan a narrow-eyed glare when he protested. So he didn't feel at all guilty about walking faster than her to get to the ticket counter before she did. Causing him to nearly miss the fact that she'd gone to a different counter until after he'd paid for two tickets. He snatched them up, stalked to where she was opening her wallet, grabbed her wrist and began dragging her to the entrance.

"You want to land on your ass again, buddy? This concrete probably isn't nearly as comfortable as the hallway at the Ritz."

He came to an abrupt halt and turned to face her. And damn if there wasn't a grin trying to break free of the expressionless face she was attempting to maintain.

"You did that just to annoy me."

"Yep."

"Brat."

He moved his grip on her wrist until they were holding hands and gave her a not- so-gentle yank until she was flush with his body. She didn't argue. She didn't even pull away. Instead she leaned in, giving him her weight, sliding her free hand up under his t-shirt.

A gaggle of teenagers wandered past and he gave a low groan as he pulled her hand away and stepped back. "You're killing me."

He handed over their tickets and they clunked through the turnstile. He spotted a shop selling funnel cakes and herded Claire over that way. "Let me take a wild guess. You've never had funnel cake before, right?"

"Uh, no. And honestly, it doesn't really seem like—"

"Trust me on this one. Really." The line was short and they were back outside quickly. He tore off a piece dusted heavily with powdered sugar, blew on it carefully, then held it to her lips. She quirked that damn eyebrow but opened up. Almost immediately her eyes closed as she absorbed the flavors.

"Mmmmm." The moan brought his cock to attention. He led her to a wide planter where they could sit and eat the treat and watch the comings and goings.

Various cartoon characters passed by in search of kids to entertain. Both of them shuddered at an especially obnoxious child being scolded by an embarrassed mother.

"Have you ever thought about having kids?" Claire asked.

"Once in a while. Long enough to think it would be nice, with the right person, but a nightmare with the wrong person."

"Sometimes I wonder about my great-grandmother. Was she a good person? What did she think about the man that her little baby grew up to be? Besides the fact that I'd be afraid to have a child my family might want access to, that's what terrifies me the most. That I would be responsible for unleashing someone like my grandfather on the world."

"I never thought about that. But like you say, you don't know what your great- grandmother was like. Maybe she was a stone-cold bitch. If she wasn't, if she was a good person, doing her best, then he was just born to be that way, no matter what she did. And what are the chances of that happening?"

"Someone wins the lottery every single day."

"Isn't it just as likely your child could grow up to find the cure for cancer? Or invent the cure for the common cold?"

"I don't know, is it? Besides, there's that whole issue of the family I already have to deal with. As long as they're a danger, then I won't be having children."

"That's not going to be a problem for long, Claire. I *will* help you with that. Both Jacob and I will. We can't just let them keep getting away with what they're doing."

"There are a lot of people getting away with a lot of things, Ryan."

"True. But we can only work on the ones we're aware of." He saw a sign reading Colossus and veered her to the line's entrance. It was a weekday so they were able to walk through most of the line, stopping about fifty people back from where a car was just pulling out, the riders grinning expectantly.

Claire's hand gripped his a little bit tighter as the cars suddenly accelerated out of sight. "Tell me why we're doing this, again?" she asked.

"Because it's fun and exciting."

"Ah. Okay."

They made their way closer, and as each car came back full of laughing riders, she began to relax again. By the time they were next in line, standing behind an iron gate, she was bouncing on her toes, craning her neck to watch for the returning train. When it came and the gate in front of them swung open, she stepped quickly to her seat, pulling down the safety bar and biting her lip.

"This ride is older than you," he said.

She frowned over at him. "Is that supposed to be a good thing or a bad thing?"

He didn't bother answering as the heavy clicks began their forward motion. Reaching over, he rested one hand over the top of hers where it gripped the bar. They pressed back into the seats as they began the steep ascent. Claire was staring straight ahead with an intense look of concentration.

"Look around you," he told her.

She jerked a glance to the side, then returned for a longer look. They were over twelve stories up, and the view was amazing. But it only lasted a moment before the car crested the hill and plunged over. He didn't watch the view. He watched her. A huge grin overtook her as her hair flew back and their stomachs dropped. When they slammed to a stop and inched their way back to the station, she turned to him, her eyes lit up in a way he'd never seen before. Joy.

They stumbled through the exit and back into the park. She turned to him, her smile still huge, her eyes still sparkling. "Let's do that again."

He had to laugh. Had to cup her face in his hands and taste the joy on her lips. She didn't hesitate to wrap her arms around him. The kiss started out strong, laced with adrenaline, and could only go up. The screams from the riders above intruded enough to remind him that they weren't alone. His own damn fault for bringing her to a public place rather than a private hotel room. Of course, he wouldn't have gotten that look, that joy, that kiss, if he hadn't brought her here. He pulled back, loving the way her eyelids fluttered open to look at him in confusion, the way the tiny flush ran up her face so fast he would have missed it if he hadn't been watching so carefully.

He leaned back down but angled past her lips to whisper in her ear, "We're going to go on another ride. Then I'm going to find a corner where I can hide us and I'm going to pull that Rabbit back out of my hat." He lifted up again, watching amusement, mortification and desire war across her face.

Finally her lips twitched. "You're not wearing a hat."

Laughing, they followed the path to the next big ride, this one newer and faster, with loops that hurtled them upside down. And when they got off, while her face was still flush with excitement, her heart still beating fast from the adrenaline, he found a corner that was dark, where he detected no video surveillance, and he covered her body with his, diving back into the kiss as if they hadn't been parted for twenty minutes, as if the rush they were feeling were directly from that kiss. From them.

When her leg began to climb up his, trying to hook around his waist, he released her mouth again. "I'm putting a spell around us. Nobody can see us and they'll walk past without stopping here."

"Magic."

"Yes. It has its uses." And with that, he held the purple vibrator he'd shown her once before, at her accidental request.

She licked her lips and looked past him, still nervous.

"I promise, nobody can see you." To make her feel more secure, he replaced her jeans with a long skirt in a flash, then eased the front up between them. Even if they hadn't been hidden, his body would block her from view.

"You've got my hands full, now," he said, one holding the Rabbit, the other her skirt. "You'll have to tell me, are you wet for me? Wet enough that I can slide this in, deep and hard?"

Her breath caught in her throat and she swallowed hard. He bent his head and licked a path up her throat. When he pulled back again, her eyes had closed.

"Are you wet for me?" he asked again.

"Yes. Please, Ryan, do something."

"Mmm, you beg so pretty. I don't think I could deny you anything when you ask me like that."

He twirled the purple head around her opening, then rubbed the whole shaft along her pussy, making sure it was good and slick before he returned to ease it inside.

"Hard. You said...hard." She gasped the last part as he was already complying, thrusting deep. He used his thumb to check that the rabbit ears were positioned correctly, then turned the vibrator on. She inhaled sharply as the ears began to buzz against her clit and the shaft inside began to rotate and vibrate. A low moan followed, but he covered her mouth with his and swallowed the sweet sound. Her hands held tightly to his biceps, her short nails digging into his shirt.

He pressed his hips in, letting her feel his hardness in contrast to the plastic inside her. She brought her hand down to scrabble at his belt. "No, honey, don't. If you do that, I won't be able to concentrate on the magic and keep us hidden."

She was panting now, her hips wriggling against his, with no room for movement, no way of escaping the constant flutter against her clit. "Too much," she whispered into his chest.

"You can take it. Take more." He thumbed the controller, adding more speed to the vibration of the shaft.

A sweet gasp escaped her and her hands went back to clutching his arms, more tightly now as she tried to push him away, get more room to move.

"Ryan."

"That's it, Claire. Let me see your face. I love to watch you give in."

She rolled her forehead back and forth, denying him the view. Her skirt was trapped between their bodies so he let go and brought his hand to her neck, sliding his thumb under her chin and tipping it backward. Her eyes were closed and lines of concentration etched across her forehead.

"We'll leave the skirt on, so next ride, when we're freefalling and your heart is beating fast, your stomach is doing a somersault and you're holding back a scream, I'll slide my hand under your waistband and see if you're wet again."

Her face relaxed as she gave in to the orgasm, her knees giving out so that he had to press himself harder into her to give her support. He turned off the device and replaced the rabbit ears with his thumb, giving a slow, careful caress as she sighed through the end of the release. He eased the vibrator out of her and let it vanish. Her head fell forward again and he wrapped his arms around her and turned, leaning against the wall and drawing her fully against him.

By the time they left the park, Claire was as relaxed as he'd ever seen her. She'd gotten into the spirit of it, even posing for pictures with some of the characters. He'd never been so glad of his ability to magically produce items as when he'd reached into his pocket and produced a camera while she was hamming it up with Sylvester the Cat. Well, producing the Rabbit had worked out pretty well too. Still, he couldn't wait to pull up a picture of her actually smiling and laughing.

She didn't even bother to argue when they got in the car and he suggested they head west to Santa Barbara and get a hotel room. They'd missed the rush-hour traffic and made good time. He directed her off the freeway before they actually reached the city, and she didn't even roll her eyes at him when he had her pull into the driveway of the Four Seasons Hotel.

"Do you think I need a room with a fireplace to be impressed by you?" she asked, doing a slow turn of the luxurious room.

"No. But I get the feeling you've had little pampering in your life. It's easy enough to do when you have the money, which in turn is easy enough to get when you're a magical being with a very long lifespan. Besides, I'll man up and admit I would have stayed here even if I was on my own." He flopped down onto the bed and studied her.

Still smiling. Still happy. He fervently hoped he wasn't about to kill that.

"Claire, do you want to talk about your abilities? I was thinking it might be a good idea to practice opening up a little bit while we're here. There won't be too many people around by the beach this late, and if it gets to be too much, we can come back here. I know you like the water, it will be soothing."

She frowned, but she didn't immediately get pissed. He forced himself to inhale when he realized he was holding his breath.

"I suppose."

He blinked. That was it?

She laughed. "Don't look so astonished. Let's take a shower first, though. And then have a drink."

He waved a hand and they were both naked.

"Now where's the fun in that?" She stepped forward and ran her hands over his chest as he rose from the bed. "Maybe I was looking forward to unwrapping you, bit by bit."

His cock came to attention in answer to her teasing. Loving her all night long was more tempting than he ever would have imagined, but not nearly as important as helping her to be safe. He scooped her up into his arms and walked them into the enormous shower, letting her turn on and adjust the water before putting her down.

Despite the looks they gave each other and the teasing touches, they managed to shower without starting anything too heavy. He gave her lounge pants and a warm sweatshirt, which she took without comment, then produced a bottle of wine from his home cellar and a couple of glasses. She hummed her appreciation of his choice, but he watched her shoulders get more and more tense as she neared the bottom of the glass. When they'd both finished, she took his hand and let him lead her down to the sand.

A long but leisurely walk brought them to a secluded area. He produced a blanket from nowhere and handed her the wine and glasses to hold while he spread it out next to a tree. He sat, leaning against the trunk, and spread his legs. She took her place between them, leaning back against his chest while he poured them more wine.

CHAPTER SEVEN

Claire gradually managed to relax back against Ryan. The waves were heavier here than they'd been in Los Angeles, the wind brisker, the air wetter. But she was warm and comfortable, Ryan a solid presence at her back, the wine a tasty reminder to relax, that nothing was going to hurt her this evening. Well, probably nothing. She hoped.

She gave a small shake of her head. Doing nothing was dangerous. The guys had convinced her of that. Hiding her head in the sand and pretending she wasn't making herself sick, as well as vulnerable, was more likely to hurt her than trying this here, now, with Ryan to help her. When her wine was gone, she set the glass down in the sand.

"So. What should I do?"

Ryan's glass appeared next to hers and his arms came up to wrap around her. "When you opened the window in Jacob's office, you were stressed and unsure and taken by surprise. I think the resulting rush of emotions, from us and the nearby houses, was overwhelming. But this time, you can concentrate on just that. You won't be worrying about walls or windows. You can focus on the flow, make sure it's a small stream, learn to direct it."

"Uh huh. And how am I going to do that?"

"Well, that's sort of like explaining how a person should use their hearing or their eyesight. You just have to dive in and concentrate, but I'll be there to help."

"Hmph." She took a deep breath and rolled her shoulders. Feeling just a bit silly, she closed her eyes and tried to remember how to *see* inside herself. Ridiculously, the smell of Ryan helped, as did the feel of him all around her. Pathetic, she thought, but could feel her own betraying smile.

Like dawn slowly lighting the night sky, she gradually began to make out her wall. Gray at first, then she remembered to look up and found the window. Once she saw it, light beamed through and she could easily make out the wall around her. It was pretty ugly. Maybe she should figure out how to make curtains. She laughed out loud at that, which almost made her lose the image, but recalled her to her body and to Ryan's. It made it easier to be in both places at once, which definitely felt better. She went to the window and, though she wasn't in the least surprised to find Ryan standing patiently on the other side, she was still somehow relieved. And pleased.

She focused her concentration on the small square, this time relying on the fact that it was her imagination, not physics, holding the window there, so who was to say it couldn't open both vertically and horizontally at the same time? Instead of opening an inch all the way up, she allowed an inch both up and down, creating a square.

The first foreign emotion she felt was pride. And hunger. Ryan's hunger. Her eyes locked with his through the window and he gave her an encouraging grin.

"Can I come in?" She heard his question both inside her head and next to her ear. The duality grounded her again, reminding her that she was in his arms, safe on the beach. A good thing, because she was starting to feel other emotions, more than hers or his. There weren't a lot squeezing through the hole, but they were hard to sort. When Ryan appeared beside her, she eased the window halfway closed. She was able to sort out his feelings from the rest.

They were the strongest, by far. It took her a minute to figure out why the next strongest was fuzzy. They were from a woman, and she was drunk. She was feeling insecure but hopeful.

"What do I do with them?" she asked in a whisper.

"You should be able to put a filter on your window. Like a screen. Once you identify someone that you don't want or need to monitor, don't let them through the window."

That sounded too easy, but she gave it a shot and was able to redirect the woman's emotional stream so that it bypassed the opening in the window.

After that, it was almost fun. She was able to examine the emotions that unerringly found their way to her and began connecting them to the outside world. Finally, she was able to open her eyes and still maintain the connection to her extra sense. A man and a woman were walking down the beach, hand in hand. She directed her attention on them and was able to sort through the stream and figure out which emotions were theirs.

"He's thinking of proposing to her," she murmured.

"You can pick up that much detail from his emotions?"

"Yes, he's practically picturing a diamond ring. He's excited and nervous and happy."

"And how does she feel?"

"Content."

"That's nice. Sweet."

"Yeah. If it were all like that, maybe it wouldn't be so bad. There's anger, further down the beach. Sadness from the hotel. Hurt from the bar."

He nuzzled her neck. "That's all part of life. Just be careful that you don't take it into yourself. You can feel their emotions, acknowledge them, but don't take them on. You'd make yourself crazy."

"It feels so rude. Invasive."

"It could be, in the wrong hands. You already know that. But trust in yourself, that you wouldn't use it against anyone who doesn't deserve it."

Shame washed through her and tightened his arms around her.

"Shit, Claire. I felt that. First, you have nothing to be ashamed of. You were a child, with no clue what you were doing when you shared other people's emotions with the family that was supposed to be taking care of you. Second, I didn't know you could project your emotions, as well as receive others."

She shrugged off the memories of her childhood and concentrated on the new information. "I didn't know I could either. Is it unusual?"

"Well, human psychics are unusual in the first place. And only some of them are empaths. I would say that very few of them can project as well as receive. So, yes. It's unusual."

"You'd think I'd have noticed."

"You've probably never actually done it before. You've been too closed-off. Here you're relaxed, open a bit, even a little trusting, I would say."

She smiled. "Yes, I guess you could say that."

His joy at her statement was like a ray of sunshine across her soul. Which, of course, made her nervous. She concentrated on keeping that feeling to herself, not because she didn't think he wasn't already aware of it, but to see if she could. She needed to learn, practice, get a handle on this part of herself she'd been ignoring for so long. But she also needed to make sure he understood.

"I'm still not sure about the future, you know."

He kissed her temple. "I know."

"I have no idea why you're even bothering with me."

"I've no idea, either. But I can't seem to help myself, so you're stuck with me, at least for a while."

"Well. That doesn't seem to be as annoying as it used to, so I guess you're growing on me."

He wiggled his hips, letting her know which parts of him were growing.

She laughed, closing the window in her mind so she could concentrate on the man holding her.

"I'm not sure I'm worth all this work you're putting into chasing me." She felt him start to answer but hurried on before he could interrupt. "I can't promise you the ending you want. Hell, I don't even know what ending you *do* want, but I want to give you something now, something that would make you happy, make this special for you."

"Honey, you're already special. Besides, I don't think you realize how much I get to be me, with you. Usually I'm with a woman who doesn't know what I really am, doesn't know my real name. It's necessary, but I don't like having to pretend. With you, I don't have to."

"I definitely get that. It's been so long since I was myself, not only am I not really sure who she was, but I have no desire to be her again. It can get a little...confusing."

He smiled against her cheek. "Yeah, I got that." He paused for a beat. "Did you know that you have a truly spectacular ass?"

She snorted. "Um, no. I wasn't aware of that, but thanks."

He slipped a hand under her sweatshirt to tease along the line of her pants. "I haven't gotten as much of a chance to admire it naked as I'd like."

"Oh. Well. We could change that, I guess."

He dipped his fingers under the waistband. "Do you trust me?"

"Mostly."

"Do you trust me with your body?"

"Mostly."

Again that lifting of lips against her cheek. Then he moved his head back and took her earlobe into his mouth, between his teeth, sucking gently, then a little bite. Her breath caught in her throat as sensation shot through her whole body.

"You don't like your bellybutton being touched."

She grimaced. "No."

"But you don't mind a raspberry and a bit of tickling now and then."

"I don't think it's ever come up before, but I guess not."

He eased his hand completely into her pants, sliding over her mound until he cupped her. She fought not to arch into him, beg him for more.

"Why don't you just tell me what you want?" she asked.

"I think you know." He circled one finger through her cream, then eased it down until he was just above the pucker of her asshole. She canted her hips, pressing her pussy more fully into his palm and her butt more firmly into the ground, out of his reach.

"Ever heard the term 'exit only'?" she asked.

"Ever heard the phrase 'don't knock it 'til you've tried it'?"

She had to laugh. "That's your argument?"

"I didn't think we were arguing." He circled the heel of his palm against her clit.

A vague sense of awareness struck her. Not anyone's emotions exactly, but the reminder that they were outside, with people nearby. She gave one last glance at the raging ocean, which somehow inspired peace. "Maybe we should take this back to the room," she suggested.

And just like that, he was holding her in his arms in the hotel bathroom, naked. The water began pouring into the Jacuzzi and a bottle of bubble bath hovered over the stream, dispensing a spicy sent into the air.

"Well. Okay, then. Magic."

"Magic."

He stepped carefully into the tub and arranged them exactly as they'd been on the sand. She had to admit, he made a pretty comfortable resting spot.

"Ryan?"

"Yeah?"

"Do you like your job? Is it very dangerous?"

"I do like it, yes. It can be dangerous, on occasion, but usually whoever we go up against is new to this world. They haven't had much of a chance to figure out the changes in their powers, their new limitations or their new strengths."

"Demons."

"Yes. And other Fae, but they don't realize yet that their magic works a bit differently here. It slows them down. Jacob's been doing this job for a long time, and he and I work well together."

"Are there a lot of Fae that don't like humans?"

"Not really, no. Just enough to make it necessary for some of us to watch out for you. Mostly it's the demons that are a problem, and they're really out of their element here. The ones with enough power to do damage are usually happier where they are, ruling their little corners of Hell."

He turned the stream off with a flick of his hand when the water was lapping over her breasts, then hit the button for the Jacuzzi.

"Mmm, that's nice. I've always thought it would be good to have a hot tub, if I ever have a yard."

"What else would you do, if you could settle down? White picket fence? Dog in the yard?"

She swallowed hard. "I, uh. I like dogs, always have. My mom had one once, but she got bored with it. When she found him playing with me one day, it pissed her off. She killed him. I stayed away from them for a long time after that. They're just so trusting. Innocent. "

He didn't say anything right away, just squeezed her tighter. "I guess you did that with people too. Stayed away to keep them safe, because of your father."

Her stomach churned but she breathed through the pain. "Not just my father. Other people died because of me. A teacher came to the house after my father died. My grades had fallen and he came to talk to my mother. Apparently it didn't go so well." She swished the water around his knee, watching the way the drops rolled down his leg, back into the tub. "I made sure my grades were average after that. No more As, no more Ds. Nothing for anyone to worry about one way or the other." She could feel his sympathy, a tiny echo of the pain she'd felt long ago. But it *was* long ago, damn it, and she wasn't going to let it rule her life anymore.

"So, anyway, a dog. I suppose, if we're talking what would I do because there really wasn't any more danger, then yes, I wish I could have a dog. A nice big one, like a Lab or a German shepherd. Actually, I suppose I'd go to the pound and get a mutt."

"I bet you'd take the ugliest one there," he said, rubbing his cheek along her hair, nuzzling her ear.

She rolled her head so that she could look up at him, gauge his statement. Of course, she could have looked inside, but she wasn't quite ready for that. His face was serious and she gave a tiny shrug. "I suppose I might."

"I hate to say it, Claire, but that's about done it. I'm pretty sure I'm falling in love with you."

Her breath froze in her chest. He bent down and opened her lips with his, teasing for a minute before pulling back. "Breathe, Claire."

She blinked at him, then turned back around and did as he suggested. He didn't seem to be in any hurry for an answer, which was good, since she had no clue what she might say to him.

He hooked his ankles over hers and bent his knees farther, sliding them both forward, then leaned back on his arms so that she was really lying on top of him. Then he tilted and a jet of water was suddenly hitting her pussy full-on.

"Ahhh." She tried to arch away, but she didn't have the necessary leverage. By the time she'd figured it out, she didn't want to move away. A thousand tiny bubbles were licking her into a frenzy. And then he moved again. Somehow he raised them up so that the majority of the stream was no longer hitting her pussy but lower, directly on her asshole.

A whole new sensation erupted and she ground her head against his chest as she fought not to move, whether closer or farther away, she couldn't really say.

And then it stopped. The water went calm and she was fairly certain she was the one growling this time. His chuckle vibrated against her chest as the water began to drain out of the tub. He gave her a little boost. "Out you go. Let's take this to the bed, shall we?"

She scowled. "Depends on what 'this' is."

He just laughed and urged her toward the room. Another wave

of the hand had the fireplace lit and the bedsheets turned down. Damn, he was handy to have around.

"How about a massage?" he asked.

"Hmph. As if I don't know where that would be leading."

"And your point is?" he asked with a shit-eating grin.

There wasn't much she could say to that and a massage did sound great. Maybe she'd fall asleep and he'd give up on his other plan for the evening. Although, after that bit of bubbly, she wasn't sure which outcome to hope for. So she'd leave it to fate and the magic of his hands. He put a dry towel on the bed and she needed no further urging to lie down, her head turned to the side so she had a gorgeous view of the ocean across the softly lit patio.

A warm drizzle of oil started at her shoulder and curled down and around her back before pooling just above her buttocks. Then his hands were on her, strong and firm, urging her muscles to melt around her bones. She may have moaned. She may have groaned. She didn't care. He drizzled more oil down her legs, then worked on her arms before returning to her shoulders and making his way back down her back. It didn't even occur to her to object when he worked her ass cheeks, digging into the muscles she'd never given much thought to.

"How you feeling, honey?"

"Mmmmmmmm."

"Is that good?"

"Mmmmmmmm."

He laughed. "I'll take that as a good. Ready to turn over?"

"Mmmmmmmm."

She was vaguely aware of him laying another towel down next to her, then he rolled her. Making no effort to engage her muscles, she just flopped over and stayed where she landed, letting him move her limbs however he wanted. When he'd arranged her to his satisfaction, he worked on her arms and legs again, then dug his fingers through her hair and massaged her scalp. This time she was positive she moaned aloud, but couldn't be bothered to care. He moved down, massaging her shoulders from the front. She forced her eyes open and watched as he moved lower, his face a mask of concentration as he carefully worked the oil into her breasts, plumping gently, his lips curling slightly as her nipples puckered fully for him. When she started to arch into his hands he moved lower, adding more oil but being careful not to drip any into her bellybutton. He smoothed it over her stomach, not pressing hard except along her sides and over her hips. A tiny bit of oil dripped onto the top of her curls and he brushed it through before looking up at her.

"Brown with just a hint of red. Auburn?"

She just nodded.

"Can I shave you? Not everything, just..." He trailed off as she waved her hand. "Sure. Whatever."

He opened his mouth then seemed to think better of questioning her.

A warm, wet cloth settled over her mound. Though she was relaxed enough she thought she could probably close her eyes and drift away, she didn't. Instead, she continued to watch his face, gathering enough energy to pull a pillow under her head so she had a better view. His concentration was absolute as he slowly and carefully drew a razor around her most sensitive areas. His fingers were gentle as he held her flesh this way and that before finally laying the warm washcloth over her again and setting the razor aside.

He looked up and seemed startled that she was watching. Then he gave a grin that was pure wolf and licked his lips. She arched one eyebrow and he took it for the challenge that it was. Removing the washcloth, he blew on her now supersensitive folds. She bit her lip to keep from crying out, then from whimpering in denial when he moved up from his position. She couldn't complain, though, when he brought his mouth to her oiled nipples. Her lax body began to hum in sensation as he sucked and pulled. She brought her hands up to run along his shoulders, loving the feel of his muscles moving beneath her fingers. Her body was fully alive now, and achingly empty .

She wrapped her legs around him and tried to urge him closer.

He left her breasts and kissed his way up her neck to meet her lips with his.

"Please, Ryan. I want you inside me," she whispered against his lips before he could claim the kiss.

"Are you sure you're ready?" he asked, but then didn't give her a chance to answer as he kissed her hard and deep.

Finally he pulled back.

"Yes, I'm ready. Please." She tightened her legs and lifted her hips into his.

He rolled over, pulling her on top of him and handing her a condom. She wasted no time sheathing him, holding him steady and driving herself down. They both moaned as her slickness enveloped him. She moved up and down, making sure to rub her clit against him with every stroke until her head fell back and she screamed her release.

She collapsed against him, panting as her inner muscles squeezed and released before fluttering to stillness. He rolled them over again and pulled out of her, still hard. She reached for him but he flipped her back onto her stomach and pulled her hips up. His hands explored her ass, sliding along the smoothly oiled skin until his thumbs were on either side of her back entrance. He pulled and she felt stretched from just that small movement.

"Ryan?"

"It's okay, honey. You can trust me with this."

She swallowed hard and then consciously relaxed her muscles again. He rewarded her with a kiss and she had to laugh. She'd never actually had anyone kiss her ass before.

"Aren't I the one who's supposed to kiss your ass, bossman?"

He chuckled. "Some other time."

And then he slid one well-oiled thumb inside her. Her body resisted for a second before she remembered to breathe, then it opened for him, accepted him. "Aaahhh."

"Did that hurt?"

"No, not really."

"Did it feel good?"

"No, not really."

"Then what did the 'Aaahhh' mean?"

She would have given him some kind of smartass answer, but he chose that moment to pull his thumb out, then push it in, starting a steady rhythm. Another dribble of oil trickled down to ease his way and before she knew it he had both thumbs inside. It wasn't exactly pleasurable, and was borderline painful. She was stretched and achy and not sure if she was ready for more.

He slid his thumbs free and she heard a small buzzing sound. She craned her neck to see a small egg vibrator. He held it out so she could see, then slipped it into her pussy. Not enough to take her anywhere on its own, it just made her want more.

"Ryan!"

"I'm here, honey."

"Do something."

"I will, Claire. I promise."

More oil and his thumbs were back inside her ass and pulling apart, stretching her in a way she'd never been stretched. It stung but she moved back into him, trying to get...something, anything. More.

She growled, and then again when she heard him laugh. His laughter cut off when she squeezed her muscles with all she had, trapping his thumbs inside. His fingertips dug into her ass cheeks and she smiled.

"All right, Claire, I'll give you more."

He pulled free from her and she let him go, wondering if she'd made a mistake. The much larger appendage prodding her backside suggested she maybe should have let him go at his own pace. But the buzzing was driving her crazy. He pushed in and she pushed back and suddenly her body accepted the head of his cock. It was tight, full, a little bit painful. She squeezed, trying to push him back out, but then relaxed and more of him slid in. She did it again, squeezing his length, then releasing, allowing him to push. It hurt, but she couldn't decide if she wanted him to stop.

"Oh, fuck, fuck, fuck," she panted.

"Claire, you're so hot, so gorgeous, so fucking tight."

She laughed at that. "What, you were expecting something else back there?"

He laughed too and then he was all the way in. The vibrations inside her turned up a level and he draped himself across her back and kissed her neck and shoulder. Supporting his weight on one arm, he used the other to reach under her and massage her breast. She pushed into him at both ends and squeezed carefully. His gasp made her smile. He let go of her and leaned back, holding her hips tightly, and began to fuck her earnestly. She braced her hands against the headboard and met him thrust for thrust.

She'd never felt so possessed, so taken, as if she'd given her body over to him. And maybe she had. She'd begged him—even egged him on. Right now, in that moment, she felt like she belonged to him. It wasn't nearly as unsettling a thought as it should have been.

He pulled her in tight and came for what seemed like forever. When he was done, he fell over her again and reached his free hand down to pull at her clit. She exploded around the egg and his softened shaft, squeezing and releasing until her knees slid out from beneath her.

He pulled out carefully and she had the vague notion of him using a washcloth on her, then rolling her under the covers and pulling her tightly into him before she was dead to the world.

CHAPTER EIGHT

They slept in and left the Four Seasons late in the morning. Again, Ryan forced himself to keep from asking where they were going and if she had a plan. She took them through a drive-thru for fast-food breakfast and they remained quiet as they ate. He stayed silent when she got on the freeway and headed north.

When she'd handed over her trash, she gave him a quick sideways look.

"You've been very un-pushy. What's up with that? Also, shouldn't you be at work?"

"My restraint amazes even me. And Jacob will let me know if he needs me. Have you ever been wine tasting?"

"No."

"Why don't we keep an eye out for a winery that looks interesting and go check it out?" he asked.

She didn't answer for a few minutes but he didn't think she was rejecting the idea. He wanted to know what she was thinking but didn't even bother wishing he could access her mind.

"You know, I don't really have a plan," she said.

"Okay."

"I've never done this before. Just, driven with no plan, no destination. No new identity. That sign looks interesting." She used her turn signal and quickly accelerated over to the exit lane.

"Jacob's working on a spell that will keep you free from psychic detection. It's not something we've ever done before, so it's taking a little work. Once that's in place, you can pick an identity you want to stay with."

"But? You said that with a clear 'but' at the end."

"But, I still think it would be better to take care of the situation, rather than continue to hide from it. These are dangerous people, they need to be stopped."

Her fingers turned white against the steering wheel. She gave a tight nod as she took the off-ramp the winery sign had indicated.

"Claire, I'm not saying you've done anything wrong. I think you've made good decisions, but now you have more options. Now you have help."

"What do you suggest?"

"I'm sure the family is under investigation by someone. I'll find out who, how much they have, what else they need. And I can make sure it doesn't get back to the wrong people," he added as her face became as white as her knuckles.

She took a deep breath and flexed her fingers. Turning into a driveway, she pulled into the first empty spot and parked. "Okay. If we can—"

The too-loud rush of an engine roaring into the parking lot behind them had a gun in his hand while his senses opened up to their surroundings to assess the danger. Claire threw the car in reverse and was squealing out of the spot before the black SUV was able to block them in. It clipped their rear bumper, but she had the car under control almost immediately. He focused on the SUV and was able to kill the engine just before his head knocked into the window when the car lurched violently to the side and jerked to a stop.

He forced his aching head forward to see a woman with a baby stroller stopped frozen where the car would have been without Claire's reflexes. A quick mental push had the woman moving for cover as Claire opened her door and he scrambled over the console to join her.

Gunfire peppered the passenger side of the car and the wall behind them. He felt a sharp sting, not painful enough for a bullet wound, probably a ricochet. The warm slide of blood tickled down his side but he refused to let it distract him. They needed to get to a place where they couldn't be seen so he could port them out. Keeping a mental eye on the fuckers in the SUV, he looked around to make sure that there were no other bystanders in immediate danger. Which was why he almost didn't catch Claire in time as she tried to bolt from the protection of the car just as another bullet slammed into it.

"What the hell are you doing?" he demanded as she struggled against the arm he'd banded around her.

"Let go of me!"

She pushed against him, forcing him to use both arms when he should be keeping all of his attention on the shooters. He followed her line of sight and could just barely see the stroller the young mother had been pushing past. Out of desperation, he tried to enter Claire's mind and was so surprised when he managed it that she almost escaped him. He tightened his grip and reached out his senses, sharing with her what he saw. The young woman had turned her ankle when she'd rushed for cover but hadn't been hit.

Sagging against him, Claire seemed unconcerned that he'd managed to break through her mental defenses, even just a little bit. He stored the elation that she was opening up to him at the back of his mind, next to the rage that he couldn't let distract him. He had to concentrate on the shooters. Sirens wailed, coming toward them quickly. They needed to get out of there, but he couldn't port them away from such a visible location. Without warning, Claire knocked him on his ass. He stared up at her in shock, one part of his brain aware that the bad guys were getting back into their car and racing away, the other trying to understand why she was pushing him to the ground. When her hands started tearing at his shirt he finally understood that she'd realized he'd been hit.

"Claire, it's okay, I'm fine."

She didn't seem to hear him so he forced the message mentally. *I'm fine, but we need to get out of here. You don't want to try to explain this to the cops, do you?*

Blinking down at him, her face pale and her eyes huge, she shook her head. He'd followed the shooters' escape with part of his mind until they'd turned the corner, racing away, but he was still cautious, poking his head above the car's hood. The baby was crying thirty feet away, but he could see the mother trying to soothe it. Someone else was poking his head out of the winery door, phone held to his ear.

Checking the nearby areas with all of his senses, Ryan found what he was looking for. He grabbed Claire's hand and pulled her up with him, stopping at the car only long enough to snatch her purse from the backseat and use his magic to clean the car and surrounding area of all fingerprints and any blood he may have dripped.

With a tug on her hand, he ran them around the back of the building, lifting a strangely compliant Claire until she could scramble over the wall and into a non-public area. He joined her on the other side and did a last double check for any windows or cameras. Finding none, he ported them to Jacob's house, figuring she'd like the comfort of being in a familiar place.

"Damn it," she exploded. "Why did you bring me here?" She held her hands up at him when he tried to answer. "Never mind, I don't want to hear how you and Jacob are hard to kill until after I've seen what's making you bleed."

He let her push his shirt up, even holding it out of the way for her. It hurt, he wasn't going to lie. Well, at least not to himself. "Honey, it's fine. This is nothing, not even a shot, really, it was a ricochet."

"Oh, for fuck's sake, Ryan, there's a bullet in you! That is not fine." She raised her voice, "Jacob! A little help here."

Jacob walked in with bandage materials and got to work. He used his magic to draw the bullet and all foreign materials out. It hurt worse than the damn thing going in, but Ryan just gritted his teeth. To distract himself, he focused on Claire, who was still alarmingly pale.

"Honey, you managed to let me into your shields. That's great, a huge step." His smile slipped a bit at the look she gave him, as if he were at least partially deranged. The handle he had on his own fury was getting slippery but he forced it back, just a little while longer.

"What happened?" Jacob asked, taping a bandage to his back.

"They were waiting for us at a winery. They're not very good, they had a clear shot at Claire, but missed."

A choked sound had both of them turning to look at her. Disbelief and rage sang equally clear in her mind, what little of it he had access to.

"Are you fucking stupid?" she asked.

He bristled but didn't have time to respond.

"I told you they don't want to kill me. They were shooting at you, damn it!" She pushed past him, not gently, and stormed out of the bathroom.

As soon as the door closed he turned to the wall and planted his fist into it. Jacob sighed but didn't say anything. Shaking his hand, Ryan tried to use the pain to help him focus and diffuse his anger. While Claire had been next to him he'd been doing everything he could to redirect it, keep it from erupting. He didn't want to scare her further, but fuck! Those stupid fuckers had shot at her! For the first time ever, he'd wanted to ignore common sense, which required that he save the fight for a better time and place, one free of innocent human witnesses. Instead, what he'd wanted to do was march over to them and rip their guts out with his bare hands. Something he was pretty sure he was capable of doing, though he'd never actually tried. Then he'd call lightning from the fucking heavens to incinerate the entrails.

"Ryan, you need to calm down. This isn't helping either of you."

"Fuck that! Do you see how close they came to shooting her?" He pointed to his side. "She may believe they only want to take her, but this bullet wasn't that far from her flesh, Jacob."

When Jacob had smoothed down the last piece of tape, Ryan brushed past him in search of Claire. He opened his senses and realized she'd made it all the way to the garage. His mind shut down. There was no real coherent thought as he ported himself to her side. No real decision making as he ignored the questioning look on her face when his hand wrapped securely around her upper arm and he spun her from the key rack she was studying. She was running from him after promising not to do so and he was done. He would take her where he knew she would be safe, deal with those trying to harm her, and when he was finished with that, he'd turn her over his knee and spank the thought of ever breaking her word to him again right out of her.

Ruthlessly, he entered the small portion of her mind she'd given him access to and sent a powerful suggestion of sleep into her brain. She sagged against him and he ported them to his homeland. Humans found it difficult to adapt to Faerie at first, and while he was furious, he didn't want her to go through that without him there to guide her. It would be easier on both of them if she slept through it. He brought them to a spare bedroom in his parents' house, rather than the empty home he owned.

Alerted to his arrival, his mother entered the bedroom as he smoothed the covers over Claire. When he turned to her, his mother blinked at whatever she saw on his face.

"I have to go. I'll be back as soon as I can, but I need you to keep her safe until I return."

"Of course, Rían, but—"

"She's going to be my wife, Mother, but she's in danger. Please, keep her safe until I get back."

He ported to the estate that he and Jacob had identified as that of Claire's uncle, mother and grandfather. They'd confirmed that the hacker activity had also originated from a source within.

Ryan, I will be there as soon as I've finished giving instructions at the office. Wait for me.

Jacob's voice in his head didn't slow him down, nor did he

bother responding. But he did allow the other man to see what he saw.

A man and woman were at work in an office, the man speaking on the phone. Though he wasn't an empath, Ryan could feel the rage pouring from the man as he slammed down the receiver.

"Fuck! The most pinpointed location we've ever received on her and they still managed to miss the bitch."

The woman's eyes narrowed. "We told them when and where. Granted, they didn't have much time to act, but how hard could it be to get an unarmed woman into the car?"

"She wasn't alone this time. Some guy was there and he returned fire."

"Not good enough, John. See that they can't talk about what happened. I don't want anyone knowing we've got a new psychic on our leash who can actually do what we need him to do."

"I'm not an idiot, Mary. They're already dead. And so will your spawn be, pretty fucking soon, if you can't figure out a way to get her here. I'm tired of this bullshit, wasting resources to bring her in."

Ryan didn't need to hear any more. Mother and uncle, conveniently alone in one room. He ported into the room, one gun in each hand pointed at the occupants. Jacob joined him, not bothering to draw a weapon.

"Who the fuck are you?" John shouted.

"I'm your new nightmare." He fired the gun, shooting the desk where Mary had been reaching her hand, presumably for a weapon. Using glamour, he made it appear as if his body was growing before their eyes until he towered over them. He produced rope from thin air and spun it around them until they were both secured to their chairs, all without moving from his position.

John's eyes were narrowed in calculation while Mary's were pinned to the door as if waiting for reinforcements.

"They won't be coming to help you. The guards on the door haven't heard a thing."

Mary's gaze shifted to him and she examined him from head to toe. "Who are you and what is it that you want?" She tried to make it sound sexy, alluring and it may have worked on some. But it just made him a bit sick inside. He needed to end this fast and get back to Claire before she woke up.

"I've already answered the first question. As to the second, I'm your daughter's lover and I take exception to her being shot at." He wanted to just kill them, but things hadn't gone quite that far yet. He had to give the human authorities a chance to deal with this scum. For now, he needed to scare them enough to ensure they would stay away from Claire.

"I don't care what you're up to here in your little corner of the world," he continued. "But now you've stepped on my toes, in my state, with my woman. Back the fuck off, or I will end you." He opened his hands and let the guns disappear back to where they'd come from. His arms remained stretched out and he pinched his fingers slowly closed, letting them each feel the corresponding closing of their throats as he restricted their ability to breathe.

Rage was flashing through John's eyes and cold calculation in Mary's. He needed to make sure they didn't think they could retaliate, even with an army. Tightening the hold, he restricted their breathing until panic finally registered. "Do we have an understanding?" He gave a small flick of his wrists and let his arms drop, releasing their throats.

Immediately both Smiths reverted to anger, fighting against their bonds. Before they had a chance to respond, he repeated the hold, this time not even bothering to raise his arms. Finally Mary ceased to fight, then John. They both nodded their heads. He wasn't an idiot, he knew they would regroup. But he would have time to figure out a plan, get the human authorities what they needed to shut the bastards down.

We hope, Jacob added. But he didn't have time to examine the doubt he heard in the other man's thoughts. He needed to get back to Claire. Time moved at different rates between the worlds, and the hour he'd spent here could have lasted anywhere from thirty minutes to five hours in Faerie.

He ported to his parents' house, directly to the room where he'd left her and staggered, nearly dropping to his knees at the pain and despair that saturated the air around him. Around her.

CLAIRE FOUGHT FOR CONSCIOUSNESS. The soft bed under her combined with the fuzzy brain that she couldn't quite get to focus was a disturbingly familiar position. Too many times she'd been drugged and strapped to a bed to force her compliance or punish her for trying to run away. Had they taken her? Killed Ryan? It was the only way she could imagine they'd gotten her away from him. Her heart nearly stopped at the idea but it gave her the strength she needed to come awake.

She was in a bed but she wasn't tied down. Cool crisp air and warm blankets surrounded her. The musical sound of heavy rain falling. Opening her eyes warily, it didn't take more than a second to realize she was somewhere she'd never been before. Panic tried to overtake her but she forced in a deep breath and tried to remember. Ryan had been shot but had gotten them to Jacob's house and sworn he was going to be fine. She'd been pissed and left them to the nursing in the bathroom, storming down the hall. Her anger had carried her to the massive garage. A light had come on automatically and she studied the interior before noticing a large key rack on the wall to her right.

Her fear and anger had begun to lessen, just the tiniest bit, when Ryan had suddenly been there, spinning her around to face him. The cold fury on his face had her blinking in shock, unable to respond when he pulled her up and then... What? That was all she remembered. Fighting to keep her breathing even and face clear of all expression in case she was being watched, she took in the room.

Prettily painted walls and curtained windows suggested it was a guest room of some sort, not a prison. She didn't know anything about paint colors and window treatments, but this was a lovely combination that was probably meant to be soothing. It wasn't working.

Rolling to her side, she slid out from the covers. And realized her shoes and socks, jeans and bra were gone, leaving her in just the t-shirt and panties Ryan had given her. Nausea threatened but she forced herself to keep breathing.

"Ryan." She hadn't meant to let the word escape, but the whisper sounded frightened even to her own ears. Damn it, she needed to be in control of herself to figure out what the hell was going on. Her hand strayed to the pendant, warm against her chest, but she jerked it away. Better to figure out what was going on before calling for help. She strode across the room to one of the closed doors and opened it. Bathroom. Really, really nice bathroom. The next door was a closet, empty apart from a robe and extra blanket. Definitely a guest room. She grabbed the robe and pulled it on, knotting the belt tightly.

That left one door, the one she'd been pretty sure led out of the bedroom. She held her breath and turned the knob, opening the door a crack. Not locked. Shutting it again, she returned to the bathroom.

It took her a whole second to realize the image in the mirror was wrong. Holy shit. *Shitshitshitshit.* She was looking at Sharon. Sharon Stanley who'd been gone for five years. The hair dye was gone, as was the relaxer, turning the dry, black mess she'd given Claire into the silky auburn curls she hadn't seen in a long time. Had never wanted to see again.

Her legs gave out, actually gave out, and she was lucky she didn't smack her chin on the counter on her way to meeting the floor with her ass. She tucked her head between her knees and concentrated on not passing out. Ryan had offered her oblivion and she'd rejected it, so she would *not* return to the unconsciousness he'd left her with. Because she could no longer deny what she'd been afraid to suspect. Ryan had brought her here. And left her here.

She grabbed the counter and hauled herself up, then rinsed her face with cold water. She avoided the face in the mirror, knowing it was more than the hair that was familiar, that her eyes would look as they had before she'd run away, before she'd become her own person. They would show the girl who'd been wholly owned and controlled by monsters.

Coming out of the bathroom, she had a perfect view of the outside through the sliding glass doors. Her heart stopped. The lush greenery and the sparkling rain nearly managed to knock her legs out from under her, again. She staggered to the doors and slapped a sweaty palm on the glass. Stunning. Terrifying. She turned her back on the beautiful sight and slid down the glass until she landed on the floor in a heap.

Faerie. He hadn't brought her to his home in San Diego. He'd brought her to a world she didn't belong in and had no hope of knowing how to survive in. Had no idea what the rules were and how she might offend. While she was rational enough to doubt he'd specifically land her in danger, in its own way this was worse than if he'd dropped her in her family's home. At least there she knew the rules, what was expected of her and how she should act. Here, she knew nothing.

Fine. But she wasn't going to sit here and wait for things to happen *to* her. No more hiding. She forced herself up and went to the bedroom door, took a deep breath and eased it open.

There was a long hallway with nobody in sight. She started down it, the stone tiles cool against her bare feet. The murmur of conversation pointed her in the right direction but the soft clatter of utensils froze her in place. There were definitely more than a couple of people here. What, had Ryan stripped her of her clothes and defenses, dumped her in bed, then called all his friends over for dinner?

It took more willpower than she liked to force her feet back into movement, but she managed it. Her face naturally fell into the blank lines she relied on and as long as no one could make out the pounding of her heart, they shouldn't be able to tell how fucking terrified she was. She rounded the corner and found the dining room.

It was crazy how familiar the tableau was. The differences should have been huge, should have destroyed any idea of similarity with her family. But the fact that the six people at the table were all damn attractive, just as she would have pictured had she been demented enough to try to imagine Ryan's family, or that the view from the room's windows was that of a sky too blue to be real and flowers she'd never seen before, did nothing to stop the association to her family's dinnertime.

Conversation stilled as the group became aware of her presence. Just like Ryan and Jacob, they were the best-looking, most perfectly put together versions of themselves that they could be. No crooked noses or thin lips. No frizzy hair or fat zits. They were elegant and fair. And yet, her mind flashed pictures of her mother and grandfather, her uncle and their lieutenants and their trashy girlfriends sitting around the table.

They'd never been allowed to miss dinner unless her grandfather was away. Until she'd turned thirteen, she'd only been invited for special occasions, but from that birthday on, she was expected to be in her chair, dressed up and silent for every dinner. It was Grandfather's version of holding court, and it was the first place she'd seen a man killed.

Watching the diners turn to look at her, she tried to remind herself that just because *her* family dinners around the table had been a special form of torture didn't mean that such was the case for most people. And who knew what it meant for Faeries. Not Claire, because she didn't know shit about Faeries. She began to imagine how she was going to hurt Ryan when she saw him again—before she disappeared from his life.

The promise of that violence was the only thing that gave her a smidgen of spine as she faced the group. That irony was something she shoved aside as a man set down his napkin and rose from the table. He gave her a slight bow. Really—more than a nod, it was a fucking bow. And how the hell was she supposed to know what the proper response to that was?

"Hello. I am Tanner, Rían's father. You are welcome in our house, Daughter."

Her stomach lurched at the title, but she was sure nothing

showed on her face. She wanted to yell and scream, to run and hide, but she would play this game.

Nodding her head, she said, "Thank you, that's very kind. Could you tell me where Ry—Rían is?"

Tanner gestured to an empty seat at the table. "Please, join us. We will tell you what we know."

Forcing her legs to take her closer, she managed to approach the empty chair. The man next to it stood and held it out for her. Though most of her still wanted to turn and run, this was the only way she was going to get any information, so she forced herself to sit.

"This is my wife, Rían's mother, Adrienne, our daughter, Tana, her husband, Ryker, my sister Sylvan and her daughter, Rielle. I'm sorry, but Rían did not have a chance to tell us your name."

"Sharon." She hadn't known she would say that, wouldn't have planned it if she'd thought ahead, but somehow, it was right. This was Sharon's world, and she would do well to remember it.

Observation was key. She needed to do this to have any idea what was going on and what she could do about it. No matter how much it sucked to be here, as far as she knew nobody was actively trying to hurt her. She needed to watch and learn.

There was no sound, but something drew her attention to the table. When she'd sat, there'd been no place setting. Now there was a plate, filled with food.

Apparently she'd made some kind of reaction, because Adrienne laid her hand on Claire's arm in a relaxing gesture and said apologetically, "We have not had a human visitor in some time, so please forgive us if we inadvertently offend you." Her voice was melodic and probably should have soothed, but Claire was too busy remembering that these people were...well, not human. She tried to give the woman a smile but it felt jerky on her lips so she gave it up.

"Can someone please tell me where Rían is?"

"He told us that you were in some danger and asked us to keep you safe until he returned." Adrienne removed her hand from

Claire's arm and poured what looked like wine into a goblet, setting it down next to her plate.

"Can you tell us what the danger is, Sharon?" Tanner asked. "Is there anything we can do to help?"

"I'm afraid he misled you somewhat. The danger is to him, not to me. It would be very helpful if you could send me back so that I can remove the danger to him." By leaving and having nothing to do with him, ever again.

Tanner frowned. "Rían said that he'd brought you here to keep you safe."

It had been a gamble, asking the question, but she needed to know what Ryan had told them and she wasn't sure how much longer she could keep from screaming. She tried to keep her voice even but she didn't have as much practice at that as she did at staying quiet. "I'm sorry that Rían has put you in this position, but he was wrong to bring me here. I don't want to be here and I'm asking you to send me home."

Asking someone to do something they didn't want to do could be an effective way of seeing their true colors. She felt a twinge of sympathy for Tanner at the confused expression on his face. There was no malice, but there was a hint of suspicion. He would not be granting her request.

"We will do our best to make you comfortable while you are here," he said, ignoring the issue. "I am sure that Rían will return shortly."

Nobody had taken a single bite since she'd stepped out from the hallway. Now they made a concerted effort to resume eating and their conversation. Rielle began to ask her a question but stopped when Claire stood and pushed her chair back from the table. All movement ceased.

"I'm sorry, but I'm not feeling well. I think I'll return to my room."

Adrienne stood as well. "Of course. I'll call the healer—"

"No. Thank you. I'll just try to get some sleep. It was nice meeting you all." She turned and walked confidently to the room, leaving Adrienne standing in the hall, watching her as she closed the door.

The panic she'd been keeping back swept over her in a tidal wave. It made no sense. Nobody had tried to hurt her, nobody had drawn blood in front of her. This was not her family and she had no reason to believe that she was in danger. But she wouldn't have believed that Ryan would take her somewhere against her will, that he would dump her on his family with no thought as to how she might react. So her intuitions and judgments about the Fae were clearly suspect.

She was losing control, could feel it slipping away, bit by bit. Rushing over to the sliding glass door, even though she just *knew* it wouldn't provide an escape route, she grabbed the handle and shoved. The door was already open a crack, but when she tried to open it more, nothing happened. Like the office door the other day, there was nothing obvious keeping it from moving, but it remained still even so. She tried to force her body through the opening but it was too small. A small shriek worked its way free from her throat. She grabbed the stupid pendant, ripped it from her neck and threw it to the floor.

A sound from outside the bedroom door had her heart racing even faster. She swung around wildly, looking for something she could break the glass with. There was a chair by the dresser. She heaved it into the glass but it bounced back, nearly knocking her over. She darted into the bathroom, unable to remember if there was a window in that room. There was, above the bathtub, but it was too high for her to reach. Running back into the room, she grabbed the chair and put it in the tub, but it was too curved and she couldn't get the chair to stay steady.

Distantly, over the roaring in her ears, she could hear crying, but she didn't stop to figure out who it was coming from. *Get out, she had to find a way out.* Back in the bedroom, she looked for something else to break the glass door. She grabbed a lamp and threw it as hard as she could but was already turning, looking for something else, when it shattered uselessly against the heavy glass. She heard running and faced the door, braced for attack.

It flung open and Tanner filled the doorway, Ryker behind him. She had no weapons, nothing to throw at them but her terror, rage and despair. So she did just that, balled them all together as tightly as she could and hurled them at the men. They staggered back, pain on their faces the last thing she saw as she collapsed to the floor, agony lancing through her head.

BED, she was back on the bed, her head too fuzzy to think, arms holding her down. She fought them, as she'd always fought them, some tiny part of her shouting, *See, I knew they would hurt me!* She could feel them battering at her mind, trying to get in, just as Jacob and Ryan had done. She went inside and filled the window she'd made with bricks, fitting them tightly so there were no cracks. Familiar soft straps wrapped around her, holding her to the bed, but they forgot the gag this time, so she screamed and screamed and screamed.

CHAPTER NINE

"Rían!" his father said, pulling him up from the floor. "Where have you been? There's something wrong with your Sharon."

Ryan was already moving but he faltered at the name Tanner used. Then he pushed it aside as he saw the straps holding Claire down. He rounded on his father.

"I asked you to keep her safe, not tie her to the fucking bed!"

His father sighed and wiped a hand over his face. *Rían, see what we saw.* He gave Ryan the memories of Claire terrified and hysterical as she thrashed on the bed, screaming.

Needing her in his arms, he used his magic to remove the straps and climbed onto the bed, pulling her into his lap, nudging aside the glorious curls he never would have imagined for her to kiss her temple.

"What happened?" he asked.

"She woke up while we were eating. She came into the dining room and we invited her to join us. She seemed...odd, but since we'd never met her, we had no idea what to expect. She joined us for a few minutes, long enough to ask me to send her back to her home, then said she wasn't feeling well and returned to her room. A few minutes later we heard a crash. Ryker and I came running and when I opened the door..." He shook his head, wiped his face again and Ryan finally noticed the man looked exhausted.

He forced himself under control. "What happened?" The tiny body in his arms was still and cold. He had to rest his hand over her heart to reassure himself that it was beating steadily.

"She threw...something at us, like a ball of fear and pain. It was overwhelming, stopped us in our tracks. And then she just fell to the floor. We got her into the bed and she started to come around, but she was hysterical, as you saw. I tried to send her to sleep but her shielding is like nothing I've ever seen before. It took about half an hour until she'd screamed her voice raw, another before she exhausted herself into sleep."

He couldn't meet his father's questioning eyes, something he'd never experienced before. "I'm sorry, Father. This is my fault. I need to take her home. I'll come back when I can and explain."

Except Claire had no home. He took her to the only place he knew that would be at least somewhat familiar to her, porting her directly to the room she'd used in Jacob's house. He heard a woof from Took as he laid her in the bed and turned to find both dog and master in the doorway.

Again, he climbed into bed and pulled her into his arms.

"You took her to your parents," Jacob prompted as Took leapt onto the bed and rested his heavy head on Claire's lap.

"Yes."

"Why is she wearing a robe?" Jacob asked as he sat on the end of the bed and reached out to touch one of Claire's feet, hidden under the covers.

"Because I'm an asshole." Shame burned his gut.

"Ah."

One of her curls tickled his cheek. He closed his eyes and pushed away the memories of her tied to the bed at his parents' house and called to mind the way she'd looked at the Ritz-Carlton. Horrible hair tangled all over the pillow, a soft, knowing smile as she watched him watching her. With the image firmly in place, he spelled her hair back to how it had been before he'd screwed up so badly.

"I was mad." He had to swallow past the lump that seemed to be taking over his throat.

"Mad at her, or those trying to kill her?"

"Both. She'd promised me that she wouldn't leave without telling me. After you patched me up, I found her in the garage."

Jacob cocked an eyebrow. "She was taking one of my cars? Surely she knew I would loan her one, or better, send her wherever she wanted to go."

Ryan sighed. "I don't think she was thinking, exactly. She was scared because I'd been shot, and just sort of...running."

Jacob looked confused.

"I wasn't thinking either." Ryan couldn't meet his partner's eyes any more than he'd been able to meet his father's. "I thought she was leaving, breaking her promise. I used the tiny crack she'd allowed me into her mind and I sent her to sleep, then took her to my parents' house. I took most of her clothes, put her to bed and told my mother to keep her safe." He brushed a hand along her cheek, down her throat. "I didn't tell my parents that if she woke up, she would be afraid. I didn't tell them that being in a strange place with a strange family would be a thousand times scarier to her than to most people. I didn't warn them that if they tried to help her by entering her mind, they would terrify her and hurt her."

Took gave a small whine and licked Claire's hand.

Jacob remained quiet for a long time. "I think that I'm going to avoid falling in love, as apparently it makes normally intelligent men remarkably stupid."

Ryan forced himself to look at Jacob, meet his eyes. "Apparently it does. I'm not sure what to do."

"I think you should give her some time. She's had a tough few days, and an even tougher few hours. Let her fight through it. She'll come around."

"Yeah, but will she want to have anything to do with me when she does?"

"Well. You might not think so. But then again, when has Claire ever done anything that we expected her to do?"

Ryan tried to give his friend a smile at that. "She told my parents her name was Sharon."

Jacob's eyes went wide. "That's not good. I think she likes being Claire."

"And she definitely doesn't like being Sharon. And I didn't give her much choice, sending her to a world she knows nothing about, a family she knew nothing about, took her clothes, changed her hair back to something she'd worked hard to get rid of..."

"It's a good thing she's not naturally violent. She'd probably try to kill you."

"Yeah," Ryan said. "Good thing."

"Perhaps she would prefer that we not sit here and watch her sleep."

"I don't want her to wake up alone and afraid."

"Took will stay."

"I don't want to go."

"That's not really the point."

"I think I love her."

"I thought we'd already established that."

"Fuck."

Jacob's only response was to lift one eyebrow. Which never failed to irritate Ryan, but for now he could only grumble a bit as he eased out from under Claire and resettled her on the bed. He gave Took a long pet, then set a small spell to alert him when there was movement in the room.

The next four hours were the slowest of Ryan's life. He forced himself to check on her only once an hour. He probably would have cheated on even that if Jacob hadn't been keeping an eye on him. Each time he eased her door open, he found her completely still, deeply asleep. It was a constant struggle to resist the temptation to see if he could get inside her head. Not only was he pretty sure that she'd sealed up tight, he knew if she sensed him there he would have no chance at all of ever gaining her trust again. Not that he thought he had much of a chance now. But the need was there, growing every minute, to see if she was in pain, and if so, to attempt to ease it.

If she was in pain, was it better to let her suffer on the chance he could be with her in the future, or try to fix it now with the almost certainty that she wouldn't let him be around to ever help her again? He was driving himself crazy, going round and round in circles. The fact was that he'd only been able to enter her mind when she'd trusted him and allowed it. Well, except for that last time, but he didn't really want to think about that. So there was every reason to think he wouldn't be able to do anything now, even if he tried. He'd give her one more hour, and then he was calling for a healer.

THE SOFT SNUFFLING of a snoring dog probably should have concerned her, but instead it gave Claire something to hold on to as she woke. She didn't need to open her eyes to know that she was back in Jacob's guest room and the comforting weight on her stomach was Took.

She figured she had about five seconds before—

The door burst open and Ryan sprang through, one second ahead of her estimate. "Claire, are you all right?"

She looked at him. Just looked. His eyes were huge and a little bit afraid. It should have made her feel good but she wasn't feeling much of anything right now. Which was a vast improvement over the last time she'd been awake. When she didn't respond, didn't yell or throw anything at him, he eased farther into the room, hands going to his pockets, looking as uncocky as she'd ever seen.

A glance at the clock told her it was afternoon but she wasn't really sure what that meant. How long she'd been...well, whatever she'd been. Asleep wasn't quite the right word. She twitched as her mind got a bit too close to remembering the screaming mess of fear she'd been. It was unsettling to discover that five years hadn't really brought her as far from Sharon as she'd thought. Ryan jerked as if he'd had to stop himself from reaching out at her slight movement. He looked a bit tormented, actually. That was just fine with her. Call her petty, but she wasn't averse to the idea of him being as fucked-up about what had happened as she was.

Took licked her elbow and she brought her hand out from the covers to give his ears a good scratch.

"Claire, I'm so sorry. I really fucked that up. I'm not going to ask you to forgive me, because what I did was unforgiveable." He freed one hand from his pocket to run it through his hair before taking a deep breath and meeting her eyes. "But I hope you know I did it because... Well, because I have deep feelings for you."

She just stared at him some more and he bit his lip. His apology wasn't helping much with the one thing she needed, which was distraction from the fact that she'd had a mental breakdown. And from the fact that she couldn't seem to feel anything right now. The despair was gone, which was good, but it didn't seem to have been replaced with anything. No anger or hurt. No hope or relief. *Nada.* Maybe that wasn't such a good thing, after all.

When she continued to remain silent, Ryan shuffled to the bed and sat down on the corner. He reached a hand out to Took and she was positive it was to keep from touching her. Smart move, although she wasn't sure she could be bothered to violence just now.

"Right. Okay. Well, you should know that when I dropped you off at my parents' place, I went to see your family. Found your mother and uncle. I, um, warned them off. Of you. Said I didn't care what they did out there, but they needed to leave you alone or they were going to have to deal with me."

She stared at him a bit harder now. He hadn't. He wouldn't. Wait, this was Ryan. He would. He had. He'd introduced mainstream evil to the supernatural. Fabulous.

"Anyway, I threatened them a bit, showed off some magic to really drive the point home."

At least now he was distracting her from her recent meltdown. But she wasn't sure she was ready to hear what new lengths her family had gone to. Gently pushing Took off her, she slid off the bed and walked to the bathroom. She didn't bother looking to see if he followed or not, because she didn't much care either way.

She stripped off the robe and ridiculous t-shirt and turned the water on as hot as she could stand it. Fear was smelly so she was probably rank. She shucked her underpants and stepped inside.

"Right." From Ryan's raised voice it sounded as if he was standing in the doorway. "We put a watch on them, and you probably saw this coming, but they almost immediately began making inquiries into finding a demon ally. I'll admit, I didn't think they'd be that stupid, but it's good news."

Finally, she heard something that brought out a reaction. Though he couldn't see it, she arched an eyebrow. How could that possibly be good news?

"Now they're coming very close to committing a crime that's under my jurisdiction. We can just keep careful watch and once they go too far, we've got them."

How many people would be hurt before they went "too far"? She soaped up her body, rinsed and repeated.

"In the meantime, Jacob's got the spell that will keep them from finding you. We can send you wherever you want and you'll be safe. Once they're dealt with, we'll let you know and you can choose to be whoever you want, wherever you want."

As she applied shampoo and conditioner, she let herself imagine that possibility. It was hard to do. Hard to see herself as free. And she kept accidentally putting Ryan in her damn imagination.

"I'll give you some time to think about that," he said before she heard the door click closed.

Free. Of course, knowing Ryan, he was still underestimating the Smiths. Was he going to kill them? That didn't seem likely. Did he think giving them some sort of magical smackdown would be enough? He would be wrong, but it might take a tragedy to prove it to him. She needed more information. But she wasn't in any hurry and stayed under the stinging hot spray until her fingers began to prune. When she got out there were clothes waiting for her on the counter. Stretchy pants and a giant sweater. Apparently Ryan was expanding his ideas for her wardrobe.

She put on the cozy outfit and went into the bedroom. The bed had been made up and looked inviting. Shaking off the temptation to go back to sleep, she left the room and wandered down toward Jacob's study. Low voices proved she'd chosen the right direction and she knocked on the door. It opened quickly and Jacob was there, pulling her into a hug. He gave her an extra-tight squeeze, then set her away from him, looking her over.

"I was worried about you."

She didn't really have an answer for that so she just shrugged.

"I've been doing some research on the Smiths. Come in, let me tell you about it. If you want to hear."

"What kind of research?" She took a seat on the couch, clearing her throat as her voice cracked. Took came to sit between her legs, his giant head resting on her thigh.

"I found out that Fred's mother named him Ferdinand. His parents died in a tenement fire in New York City when he was eleven. He spent time in and out of orphanages until he was eighteen and changed his name when he was twenty-one. Records are sparse, but there's pretty clear indication he was well-established in his life of crime by that time."

"And the Smith?"

"Most likely given to his parents by the immigration officials."

She nodded. It was vaguely interesting but not what she'd come to find out.

"How much damage will they have to do before you can step in? And how are you going to stop them?" She didn't look at either of them as she asked, just scratched behind Took's ears.

"Based on the information that they're researching, they're about to attempt to make contract with a demon. Just doing that makes them guilty, but depending on what the contract is will determine how guilty. They don't—"

He broke off suddenly as Ryan moved to stand in front of Claire. She didn't think he even realized what he'd done.

"They've triggered a magical alarm at the office. They're—" This time Jacob broke off as Claire slapped her hand around Ryan's wrist. "They're about to attack, Claire, we need to go." And he left, leaving Ryan to deal with her.

He turned to look at her but she stopped him before he could say anything.

"You're not going to tell me no, so you might as well save time and just go."

His lips tightened in annoyance, or maybe outright anger. She didn't know and didn't care. She was responsible for this and if there was a chance she could help, she was going to be there to do so.

That curious sense of being nowhere rushed through her and she was suddenly in Ryan and Jacob's office. Alone. She blinked as Took appeared between her and the doorway. The dog wouldn't hurt her, but he might be able to keep her from opening the door.

Three quick steps brought her to the east-facing window. She yanked the blinds and looked out but could see nothing moving. Yet. Going behind Jacob's desk to the window facing north, she was a little more careful, easing a couple of slats open so she could peer out. Black-suited men were creeping toward the building, and they appeared to be heavily armed. Had Jacob and Ryan warned the employees? Or were they attempting to stop the bad guys and send them away without anyone ever knowing about it? And was there a single damn thing she could do to help?

Fear rolled into her, filling the emotionless void of earlier. If anyone was hurt, if Ryan was hurt, it would be because of her. They were here because of her. She let herself remember being in Ryan's parents' house, the terror she'd felt, the pain and betrayal. Letting it build along with her fury as she watched one man raise what looked a hell of a lot like a grenade launcher and aim it toward the front doors, she also remembered how she'd lobbed those feelings at Tanner. Remembered how she'd opened her window and poured the feelings out. She did it again. Only this time, she projectile vomited the feelings, getting as much speed and distance as she could. Sending everything she had, every bit of the feelings she'd been pushing down and away since before she'd woken up.

The guy holding the big weapon dropped and screamed, clutching his head. The man next to him went down too, unconscious. Two more wheeled around, looking for a target. Jacob appeared, followed quickly by Ryan, and they attacked. It wasn't a battle. It was barely a fight. Within two minutes they had all four men disarmed and secured. Claire felt as if there were a knife stabbing through her eyeball. Her knees gave way and she collapsed to the ground. She didn't go unconscious, exactly. She could feel Took come over, put his big nose in her face and lick her neck. She just couldn't seem to do anything about it.

CHAPTER TEN

"Claire, I swear, if you do anything like that again I'm going to spank you until you can't sit down for a week."

Ryan's voice sounded far away, but she was pretty sure those were his arms picking her up and holding her tight.

"She's in shock. Put a blanket around her." That was Jacob's voice. He sounded distant, too, but while Ryan's words had been angry, his voice had been afraid. Jacob just sounded pissed.

Someone shoved a straw to her lips so she figured she might as well see what it was. Apple juice? She hated apple juice. Normally she would keep drinking anyway, because letting someone know what she liked or hated was a bad idea, but wasn't she supposed to be sort of free now? Despite the fact that men with guns had come to the office, she was stuck on this whole free thing, and fuck if she was going to let it disappear this quickly.

Leaping to her feet proved not quite as easy to execute as she'd imagined. She struggled free of the blanket she hadn't noticed and sort of rolled off Ryan's lap and onto the floor. He kept hold of her enough to keep her from falling, then let her go once she was safely on the ground. When she immediately jumped to her feet, he caught her as she just as immediately lost the ability to stand. He set her on the couch then backed away.

"Just give yourself a minute. You expended a lot of energy." Ryan sounded tired. She looked up at him, but it wasn't tired she was seeing. It was sad. She felt bad for half a second, then remembered that he was the bad guy here, not her.

"What did you do with them?"

"Turned them over to the police." Ryan dropped down on the other end of the couch.

"That was fast."

"Yes, well," Jacob said. "As much as you like to pretend otherwise, we do know what we're doing. We've been doing it for some time, and rather well."

She stared at him. He was pissed. Jacob was pissed at her for coming here? When she'd stopped those shits from firing on his building? "I—"

"No, Claire. I'm not interested in hearing your excuses."

That got her blood pumping and she stood, mostly steady this time. "My excuses?" she shouted. "I stopped that guy—"

"You interrupted the plan that Ryan and I had, and you risked yourself to do it. Butting in to these situations—"

"Butting in? I'm already in the middle of the fucking situation, Jacob. It's me they're after. My fault if someone gets hurt while they're—"

"That again. Everything they do is not your responsibility. Claire, if they kill anyone, it's their action, their fault, their responsibility. All we can do is try to stop them." He took a deep breath then pinned her with an intense look. "If you had alerted the police to a hostage situation, once the S.W.A.T. team arrived would you butt in and try to fix things yourself?"

She blinked. "Um. No?"

"Of course not. You would leave it to the professionals."

Well, if he was going to put it that way. "Jacob, I..." *Can't think of a good response to that.* She sat down on the couch again. "I'm sorry."

This time it was Jacob who blinked. Then exchanged looks with Ryan.

She rolled her eyes. It wasn't like she'd never admitted to being wrong before. She just tried not to make a habit of it.

There wasn't much to say after that. The guys did a bit of work while she dozed on the couch, then they went home. She shook her head. Back to Jacob's house. If she let Ryan hold her hand and squeezed her eyes closed tight when Jacob cast the spell that would supposedly keep her safe from psychics, well, then fine. Maybe she was a wuss. She was okay with that. He didn't complain when she pulled her hand free, just gave her a tiny squeeze and a sad smile that made her look away.

She found her purse in the guest bedroom and brought it into the study, spreading around the various IDs. It was time to choose who she was going to become and where she was going to go. Her hand hovered over them before picking up the packet for Tara Small. Cut a few inches off her hair, have it dyed a light brown, pick up a pair of glasses with no prescription and she'd be set. Usually she left the state when changing locations, but maybe she'd throw them off a bit by staying in California. She could go inland, maybe the mountains. Go even more off her beaten path and pick a small town. Smart or stupid? Could she even tell the difference anymore?

Apparently not because even though she was mad at Ryan, even though he'd betrayed her and she couldn't possibly trust him, her body ached for him. She found herself glancing at him constantly, listening to him when she couldn't care less about what he was talking about, reaching for him when he was close enough to touch. Definitely not smart.

She needed to pick her place, get out before she completely lost her mind and kissed him like she kept imagining. For once, he was behaving. He seemed...contrite. And every so often she caught a look that she could only describe as hopeless. It did strange things to her stomach. And her heart.

"Fresno," she blurted out. Yes. Fresno. She didn't want the soothing view of oceans or the aching beauty of mountains. She'd never been to Fresno before, but she remembered on the map that it seemed to be out in the middle of nowhere. Who knew, maybe that was a completely inaccurate belief. Didn't matter. She'd find out when she got there. And if it wasn't what she wanted, whatever the hell that was, she could move on, keep trying, until she found somewhere... Well. Somewhere.

"Fresno," Jacob repeated.

"Yes. Maybe you could put me at the bus station. I should be able to get downtown and find a hairdresser from there."

He tried to hold her gaze but she wasn't having any of that. She stared through him until he sighed and nodded. "Fresno."

She gathered her things and put them back in her purse. "If you want to give me back my original outfit, I can leave this one in the bedroom."

Ryan spoke quietly. "You can keep it. Or if it's not appropriate for the new you, you can show me what you need."

"No, this is fine. I just wasn't sure if you needed to return it somehow." Not that she'd bothered to wonder that before, but then, she'd ignored a lot of things that she should have paid attention to. Mostly about herself.

She looked around, as if she had anything she might be forgetting, then shrugged her purse over her shoulder. "You'll let me know when the family breaks enough laws that you can take care of them?"

"If you'll take the necklace back, it will turn warm when we need to contact you. Hold it and think of us and we'll be able to come to you. Just make sure you're somewhere we can't be seen, unless it's an emergency."

She stared at the pendant Ryan held out. When he started to drop his hand, she gave in to impulse and snatched up the necklace. She shoved it into her pocket.

Blinking her eyes against a sudden bizarre wetness, she nodded her head. "I'm ready."

Jacob came and gave her a hug. She found herself clinging to him and pulled herself back. He put his hands on her shoulders, keeping her still as he studied her. This time she forced herself to meet his eyes, hoping he would somehow miss the turmoil she was feeling.

"It doesn't need to be an emergency to use the necklace. And you know how to contact us otherwise—phone, email."

She nodded. He kissed her forehead and stepped back.

Ryan came to take his place in front of her. "I am sorry."

"I know."

He held his hand out and after a small hesitation, she took it. The damn roiling in her stomach increased as he brought her knuckles to his lips and gave them a small kiss.

"Goodbye, Claire."

Whether she was going to answer him or not didn't matter as she blinked away. Reappearing in another bathroom stall, this one not nearly as nice as the Sheraton's, she nevertheless sank to the seat behind her so that she could bury her head in her hands and cry.

It probably wasn't too unusual to find crying women in the terminal's restroom, but when she heard the door open and the chatting voices of two or three women coming in, she stood up and wiped her face. She waited until they were in their own stalls before escaping hers and going to the sink. Cold water helped a tiny bit but she didn't check her reflection in the mirror. No need to see what it would show her. Besides, she didn't want to see Claire anymore. It was time to become Tara. She went out and found a pay-phone with most of the phone book still intact. Choosing a hair salon was a stab in the dark, but she memorized a couple of the names and addresses and went out to find the route map.

Three hours later she was cut, dyed and ready to go. She stared in the mirror at the stranger, slipping on the glasses from the drugstore. Tara's hair was a lot better than Claire's had been, which was nice. She tried not to think of Ryan running his hands through it. Besides, he'd want it to be different. He'd want Sharon's hair. Dumbass.

The hairdresser had been happy to babble on about apartment prospects and which neighborhoods she should avoid, so it was only a few more hours before she was filling out an application for an apartment. Going with her new theme of making decisions even knowing they weren't the smartest choice, she picked a place that was nicer, and therefore more expensive, than she normally would. She found a Super 8 motel, grabbed some fast food and checked in. Back to life as usual.

A waitressing job at a local diner was exactly what she needed. Busy enough to keep her brain occupied and her body exhausted so that she returned home each evening with barely enough energy to drop into bed. But not busy enough to keep her from dreaming. Night after night she relived heaven in Ryan's arms and woke up aching and empty. It was bad enough that she almost gave in to the advances of a regular who had doormat written all over him. Just her type. But she retained enough of her sanity to know it would make things worse, not better.

After three weeks on the job taking every shift they would let her only to go home to restless nights, she was nearly ready to drop. She was arguing with the manager about wanting to work the next day when the pendant between her breasts began to warm. She stuttered mid-sentence, then confused the poor guy by giving in to his demand that she go home and not come back for two days, nodding vaguely when he admonished her to get some sleep. Pulling the pendant free of her shirt, she held it tightly in her fist.

Part of her wanted to run the four blocks to her apartment and part of her wanted to stay outside, in public, where they wouldn't come to her. Where she could remain ignorant. Stupid. But her feet carried her home at a slightly rushed pace and it wasn't long before she was in the sparsely furnished apartment.

She took a deep breath and held the rose a little bit tighter. She didn't have to think of Ryan, because she never really stopped unless she was being run ragged at the diner. She just had to direct those thoughts to the jewelry. It warmed even more and she thought she felt a slight tingle, then it cooled. And he was there.

Pretending she didn't feel her heart lurch or her stomach clench was useless as her hand automatically reached out to touch him.

Welcome him. Damn it. She fisted her hand and returned it to her side, hoping he hadn't noticed.

"Cl—" He stopped himself and frowned. "I don't know what to call you."

She didn't know either. It had never been an issue. Usually she had no trouble letting one identity go, but becoming Tara had been the hardest transition she'd ever made. "Sharon. You can call me Sharon."

He flinched. "No. I'm sorry, but I can't do that." She shrugged. "Then call me Tara."

"I'll try."

"What's happened?" She glanced down and saw that his fists were opening and closing, over and over. It made her realize that her nails were digging into her palms. Looking back up she found that he was scanning her up and down, making sure she was okay. Or else he was strangely fascinated by her diner uniform of jeans and a purple t-shirt with a huge yellow happy face on it. It should irritate her, but it didn't. It pleased her that maybe he'd missed her as much as she had him.

He looked away and gestured to the second-hand couch. She sat on one end and he took the other, giving her as much space as he could. Damn it.

"You won't be surprised to hear that your family surpassed our expectations for how far they were willing to go and how much power they wanted. They tried to double-cross a class two demon, which is about as stupid as you can get. Of course, the demon was planning on double-crossing them too."

"Class two?"

"Usually only class three demons bother coming to this realm. They don't have enough power in their world to do what they want to, so they figure they can come here, where they're more powerful than the majority. It rarely works out for them, which means it's usually only the stupider ones who try. Somehow your mother got in contact with this class two demon. Luckily they targeted some drug dealers for their initial foray, which means Jacob and I didn't feel we needed to step in until they'd committed themselves. A few drug dealers died, we had to kill the demon. Your uncle..." Ryan shook his head. "John wouldn't stop. I...had to kill him."

He looked at her, waiting for a reaction, but she had nothing to give him. "I'm not quite ready to celebrate yet, if that's what you're waiting for. But I'm not upset, either."

"Right. We decided to wipe Fred and your moth—Mary's memories."

What? "What? You think they'd just stop being criminals? Or did you wipe out their whole lives?"

"We were going to wipe out the demon information and get enough evidence from them to make sure they were sent away for good. Fred was actually in the early stages of Alzheimer's. Jacob wiped all traces of the last couple of months and sort of helped the dementia along. He's in a state-run facility now. But your mother didn't react well. She had a stroke and died."

Maybe she was having some difficulties herself, because she felt sort of numb. "So, it's over. They're gone."

"They're gone. The organization is dead. The higher-level lieutenants have been arrested and didn't know about the supernatural stuff. We'll keep an eye on them to make sure nobody mentions your name, but...it's over. You're free."

She tried to think of something to say. Something to do. Something to feel. But she had nothing. The numbness was inside and out and she could only look at him. He lifted his arm and brought his hand out to touch her, slowly, giving her time to yell at him or hit him. But she just sat there and waited.

His fingers touched her cheek, tracing a line from just below her eyes to near her chin. Lifting the finger up he showed her the tear he'd gathered. It was enough to break through the icy hold that was strangling her. She threw herself at him and when he didn't hesitate to catch her, when he folded her into his arms and wrapped himself around her, tucking her head beneath his chin and murmuring into her ear, she began to sob.

He tightened his grip and said who knows what. All she cared about was that she felt safe and secure. It felt like what she imagined home was supposed to feel like.

She cried until she was just about numb again, only this time it didn't feel as if the weight of the whole world was pressing down on her. This felt more like a waiting. Like she was ready to live her own life, her real life, and fill herself up with those feelings. And she wanted to start now.

As surreptitiously as possible, she wiped her nose on her sleeve. Then she nuzzled it into Ryan's neck, breathing in deeply. Mmmm. She darted her tongue out for a taste and smiled when his breathing hitched. He tasted warm, like sunshine, and she wanted more. Pulling herself up a bit she nipped his chin then licked a path along it until she reached his ear. Sucking the lobe into her mouth had his arms holding her even tighter. Then he tried to push her away. Oh, hell no.

"Honey. This probably isn't a good time. You're emotional and—"

He broke off when she bit down. She wondered if he was aware that his hands had gone from pushing on her shoulders to caressing her back.

"Take our clothes off," she whispered. When nothing happened she bit him again. "Now."

If he hadn't complied she probably would have had a meltdown of doubt and insecurities. But they were suddenly naked and all was right with her world. Her hands came up to feel that wonderful skin. Up his back and down his shoulders and chest, all the while she played with his ear until he growled, fisted his hand in her hair and drew her mouth over to his.

But he didn't take and plunder as she expected. He sipped and nibbled, teased and tortured. When he drew away enough to lick a trail on her cheek, she knew she was crying again. Damn it.

She pulled back. "I don't know what's wrong with me," she choked out. "Nothing's wrong with you, Claire. Nothing at all."

She laughed and hiccupped. "Liar."

"No." He kissed her again. "You're perfect. Perfect for me."

"Then you're crazy." But she couldn't keep herself from meeting his lips, over and over.

"Maybe so. I'm okay with that."

"And you're still in trouble."

"I'm okay with that too. As long as I'm here and you're here."

She didn't want to think about that right now either, so she slid out of his lap and onto the floor, kneeling between his knees, running her hands down his chest and stomach to the cock that was hard and ready, for her.

"Claire..."

"Hmmm?" she hummed absently, stroking his flesh, watching it grow.

"You're upset. We shouldn't..."

"No?" she asked when he trailed off. She leaned down and licked the top of his cock like an ice-cream cone. "You don't want this?"

"Ah, fuck."

She moved her hands down lower and this time went for the Popsicle angle, engulfing the head with her mouth, sucking hard until her cheeks hollowed, her tongue in constant action.

"Fuck!"

She hummed again and he tightened his legs around her. He threaded his fingers through her hair, but remained gentle. Releasing him with a last kiss to the head, she nibbled her way down the side, freeing one hand to explore his balls. She bounced them a little and smiled when he grunted, then tried to see how far around his shaft she could curl her tongue. She ran it up and down, covering as much of him as she could, before pulling the tip into her mouth again. This time she sucked him in as far as she could. When his hips bucked up she took more, fighting her reflexes until she couldn't breathe, then easing back. She drew him all the way out then tongued that delicate spot under the head.

"Claire!"

She took a deep breath and went back to it, pulling him in deep then scraping her teeth along his shaft as she pulled back, again and again until his hands fisted in her hair and he came with a sharp cry.

He collapsed back against the couch and she licked around him, cleaning him up then moving to his abs and that hipbone she loved to nibble on. His hands cupped her face and she let him draw her back for a kiss.

Without warning he spun her around until they'd reversed positions, her back hard into the couch, her knees up over his shoulders, his lips closing over her clit. She arched up into him but he settled his hands hard on her hips.

"Don't move."

Her whole body clenched in reaction, then shuddered as his tongue thrust into her channel.

"Fuck!" It was all she could think to say as sensation rocketed through her body. She brought her hands up to her breasts and brushed her nipples.

He growled against her sensitive flesh. "No. Mine. Put your hands back and don't move."

Resisting was only a fleeting thought. She put her hands where they'd been and he eased back, teasing and nibbling, moving his hands up to squeeze her breasts and pluck at her nipples. Much better than her own fingers. She clenched her thighs against the need to move, her restless hands going to his hair. He couldn't complain about that, right? He growled again as she threaded her hands through the silky strands, careful not to pull, but he didn't say anything.

He pulled her clit between his teeth, stabbing it with his tongue. She came in a small burst, her empty cunt clenching hard.

"Ryan, please."

Two fingers circled her opening. "More, Ryan, more."

He thrust his fingers in hard and deep and she came again, squeezing him as he continued to lick at her clit. When she stopped spasming, he removed his fingers and put them against her back hole. Teasing her with her own slickness, he eased one finger inside. Too much. It was too much, but not enough. His fingers pulled out only to be replaced by something hard. That damn magical ability to produce whatever he wanted. The plug, or whatever it was, eased inside her ass, one knob, then a bigger one, and another, until she felt stuffed full.

"Ryan!"

This time she gave in to the need and tugged on his hair. He let her go, surging up to meet her mouth with his, her knees now pressing up near her shoulders. He filled her in one quick thrust, tongue and cock at the same time. She wanted to squeeze him to her, rock her hips, something, but she couldn't move. Completely at his mercy while his hips stayed still and he devoured her with his tongue.

At least now she could bring her hands up. She scored her short nails down his back and he gasped into her mouth, his hips jerking finally, driving him farther into her. He began to pump, ignoring her wordless demands for hard and fast, steadily rocking in and out while his tongue twisted and twirled, dancing with hers. She pulled her mouth free from his, panting for breath.

He moved his lips to her neck, sucking hard. Her ass squeezed around the plug, her pussy tightening on his cock. His pace increased, faster and faster until he was grunting with every thrust. He reached down with one hand and fingered her clit. Electricity shot through her already overwhelmed nerves and she flew. Her head fell to the side, her lips against his arm, which was braced beside her head. She gave it a tiny bite. He froze above her and she watched him, neck straining, muscles clenched, eyes tightly closed as he came inside her.

HIS KNEES HIT the floor with a dull thud that Ryan didn't really feel. Claire's legs slid from his shoulders. The roaring in his ears gradually dimmed and he realized his eyes were closed and his head pillowed on her stomach. Her fingers had found their way back to his hair but they were barely moving. He turned his head to kiss her belly, then opened his eyes and looked up.

She was relaxed, eyes closed, slight smile teasing her lips. She was beautiful. There was no way he could let her go, no matter how little he deserved her. He just wasn't strong enough to walk away. The fact that she'd let him fuck her nearly into unconsciousness gave him some hope that he wouldn't have to become a pathetic stalker to achieve his goals.

He heaved himself to his feet and lifted her into his arms. She didn't resist, just snuggled into his chest and let him carry her down the only hall to what he presumed was the bedroom. Kicking open a door that was mostly closed, he found the bed. He set her down on her side and lay behind her, his still half-hard cock sliding easily back into place. She moaned and clutched the arm he'd wrapped around her waist.

Easing her hair back, he nuzzled her cheek. She turned into him, offering her sweet lips.

"I love you," he said. It wasn't as hard as he'd imagined.

A flicker of pain passed over her before she turned, resting her cheek back on the bed.

"You don't even have to trust my words on that, you can open up and see it for yourself."

"That doesn't mean you're right for me."

If he hadn't been holding her naked and relaxed in his arms, it might have scared him off.

"People make mistakes, Claire. You do, I do. You will, I will." She wasn't wrong. But neither was he. "You love me, too, you know. Otherwise, this wouldn't hurt so badly ."

This time she did tense up. Which only served to squeeze his dick tighter. She gasped.

"Don't you see, Claire? We are right for each other. We love each other, and we make mistakes and we fuck up, but at the end of the day, we come back to each other."

"How can you love me when you don't even know me? I don't even know me! I don't know who I'm going to be, or how to stop being the person on the run."

He flexed his hips, easing out and pushing back inside. Proving her wrong. "I know who you are now, and that's what matters. Not who you used to be, but who you are now. We're all changing, Claire, every one of us. The trick is being with someone who changes with you. We can change together, grow together, *be* together. It's normal."

"What the fuck do I know from normal, Ryan? I've lived a life about as far from normal as you can get. Hell, I've never even been in a relationship. I'll just fuck this up, and it will hurt both of us."

He bit his lip to keep from grinning. She was so his.

"Then you know what not to do. As for the rest, you just do what feels right. Making mistakes and fighting is normal. I'm not making excuses, what I did was beyond normal, beyond acceptable. But we were in pretty fucking extraordinary circumstances, and I thought I was going to lose you. I'm sorry. I'll say it again and again until you believe me. I'm sorry."

"I believe that you're sorry. But how can I believe that it won't happen again? That it won't hurt so bad, again?"

"I wish I could promise I'd never hurt you again. I can't. But I can promise that giving up on this, on us, living without what we have just to keep yourself safe..." He shook his head. "Besides. You're too late. It already hurts, thinking of spending another day without you. Is that just me, Claire? Did you have no trouble becoming Tara, leaving Claire behind? Leaving me behind?"

She shuddered. "It sucked, and you know it."

"Don't trade potential future pain for pain right now. Not when there's the possibility of so much between us. Give me a month. Live with me for a month, just normal life, no more drama. At the end, if you want to walk away, I won't try to stop you."

"How can I risk it?"

"That I'll stop you?"

"No, that I'll love you."

"You already love me."

"That I'll want to stay."

"You already want to stay. Otherwise you would have left by now."

"That it will be real."

"It's already real. You're just scared, and you have every right to be."

"It's already too late. Walking away won't save me."

His throat tightened. "No. You're already mine. And I'm yours. You just have to face up to it. Give in to it."

"It's not easy."

"No. But when the hell has your life ever been easy?"

She snorted. Then eased her hips back and gave a little twist.

He gasped into her hair, slid his hand down to her clit and flicked it. "I love you, Claire."

"I like the way that sounds. Maybe I'll keep Claire, she's been pretty good to me."

"I know I'm keeping her. Whatever name she goes by. Wherever she wants to live, whatever she wants to do." He clamped his teeth down on the juncture of her shoulder and neck.

"Ahh. You said a month. You would leave, if I told you to."

He bit then suckled the spot. "I'll just have to make sure you don't tell me to."

"Say it again." Her inner muscles already quivered with the start of her release.

"I love you, Claire."

She gave a long sigh as she came around him. He pumped into her one more time and joined her.

"I love you too, Ryan."

It was barely a whisper, but it was enough. More than enough. He tightened his arms around her, keeping her close as they drifted off to sleep.

EXCERPT

Bound by Sunlight
By KB Alan
(Available now)

Kyriana Price has spent nearly a year trapped at her evil day job. And she does mean evil. Her boss is a mage bent on power and lets nothing stand in the way of his quest to gain more of it. When she sees Connul Graysn wielding a flogger at a BDSM club, she formulates an escape plan that will require his considerable skills—as a mage and as a Dom. Going to another mage for help might not be the best plan, but it's the only one she's got, and at this point, she's willing to try just about anything.

The last thing Connul expects when he finds an intruder in his house is that he'll soon have her chained in his bedroom, her lovely body marked by his paddle. But she's begging for his help—how can a gentleman refuse? As they learn to trust each other, he begins to realize that the only thing he's not willing to do for her is let her go.

EXCERPT

"You've never been bound?" he asked, picking up the straps of her tank top.

"No." It was more of a breath than a whisper, but he seemed satisfied with her answer. She felt a soft spark against her shoulders and looked down. He'd severed the straps of her top, which were left to dangle above her breasts. Magic. He'd used magic. A tiny niggle of fear tried to work its way through her. He seemed to know and brought his warm hands back to her face, tilting her head up enough that she knew she was supposed to meet his eyes. Why did she find that so difficult? She forced herself to follow his unspoken demand.

"I will not harm you tonight. Not with magic. Not with anything else. I will bring you pain, but only as much as will pleasure you. Do you understand?"

She saw patience and assurance in his eyes, wondered what he saw in hers. Shame washed through her now—that she had come to him so unprepared, unworthy. He shouldn't have to deal with a novice when he was used to those at the club. His fingers on her chin tightened.

"Do you understand?" he asked again.

"Yes."

He knew there was more, she could see it in his face, see him trying to figure it out. As long as he didn't ask, she wouldn't have to admit to her insecurities. He cocked his head as he studied her.

"What distressed you now?"

She wanted to look away. The feeling of easy surrender had vanished. But she had to answer him. Had to keep meeting his eyes. Not just because of the compulsion, but because she had asked for this. Asked him to help her. He deserved to have as much of her courage as she could muster.

"I'm sorry. I'm not very good at this. I don't know what to do."

"You don't have to know what to do. That's what I'm here for.

You'll do what I tell you, when I tell you. Won't you?" His voice was hard, uncompromising.

"Yes."

"Then there's nothing for you to fail at. It's my responsibility to make sure this goes right, not yours. Your only responsibility is to tell me if I go too far." He stepped closer, allowing his heat to envelope her. She felt moisture gather in her pussy and it got a little bit harder to draw breath.

"Let's start over." He pulled her chin up higher now that he was closer to her. Her neck ached a little at the strain. It felt...good.

"Do you believe that I won't harm you, even though I have every intention of bringing you pain?"

"Yes." She didn't know why, and it might be foolish, but she believed him. It was the reason she was here.

He rewarded her with a small kiss to her lips. She opened for him but he drew away. She sighed.

"Do you believe that I will bring you pleasure?"

"Yesss."

This time he smiled as he kissed her. She tried to chase his lips, but his hands kept her in position.

"Do you understand what you're supposed to do?"

Uh oh. What was she supposed to do? Hadn't he just told her—oh.

"Yes." Another kiss, she wanted another kiss. A real one this time, damn it.

"Tell me."

"Whatever you tell me to do." She parted her lips in preparation. She would have to be fast this time.

"And?"

No kiss? What was he doing to her?

"And...umm. Oh, and use my safe word if you go too far."

"Good girl." He met her lips with his, but it wasn't gentle this time. He thrust his tongue into her mouth, taking what she had tried to take, giving what she needed. She whimpered when he pulled back.

"Tell me your safe word again."

She didn't want to, didn't want to ever say that word again. He seemed to understand.

"Choose another word. It doesn't need to be that one. Shouldn't be something you don't want to say."

"No, it's all right—"

His fingers tightened against her skin again, reminding her who was in charge. He wasn't asking. He was telling.

"I, maybe...Snowball!" God, all she could come up with was her childhood cat's name. Was he smirking at her? She narrowed her eyes at him but his face had gone expressionless again. He leaned down and gave her another quick kiss. Then he let her go, stepped back, taking his heat with him.

"If you use your safe word, I'll stop what I'm doing so we can talk about it. Don't be afraid to use it, it doesn't mean I'm going to send you away."

She managed to nod her understanding.

"You have a lovely body."

She didn't. Her size eight curves weren't quite proportioned the way she'd like and—

He smacked her ass and she jumped as much as the chains would allow, which wasn't much at all. Why she should be shocked she had no idea, but she looked at him for an explanation.

"You." He put his hands on top of her head then ran them over her face, rubbing her eyebrows, exploring her cheekbones, tickling her ears and caressing her chin.

"Have." Her skin tingled as his hands moved down her neck to her now heaving chest.

"A lovely." His fingers molded to her breasts, giving a sharp, barely painful squeeze before continuing their journey.

"Body." He reversed his hands so that his fingers led the way over the curve of her stomach to the juncture of her thighs. He folded his hands along the curve, careful not to touch the part of her that needed touching the most.

"Oh," she managed to whisper. Her whole body shuddered at his

EXCERPT

intense look and careful caress. The desire in his words and his eyes did more to relax her than anything else he could have done. She didn't realize how worried she'd been about the fact that by presenting herself to him, rather than having him choose her, she would have a hard time believing he wanted this, even a little bit.

She looked down at her top. He was running a finger down its center, from neck to hem. As his finger slid past, the fabric parted, splitting down the middle. It was almost like a breath of heat, but maybe she was imagining that. It didn't take long for the whole top to fall away.

Her naked breasts were damp with sweat, her nipples somewhat swollen. He ignored them and brought his finger to her pants, performing a similar magic to remove them in less than a minute. He took a step back, observing her dressed only in plain cotton panties. It looked as if he was fighting a smile. She tried not to blush and failed. Why hadn't she dressed up for him? She had the clothes, had been provided with the types of outfits that were supposed to entice him. Black leather, lace garters and more. Much more. It wasn't that she didn't like them, but she would have felt like a spy wearing them, like a fraud. So she'd come in the most Kyriana-like clothes she had.

He walked behind her, hooked a finger in the waistband and snapped the elastic against her skin. It didn't hurt, but it startled her. She hung her head as she tried to fight off the shame and misery working their way through her.

"Just checking to see if your name was embroidered in the back." His teasing words were spoken against her neck. She choked on her laugh as his lips moved down her neck to the top of her spine, where he bit, hard.

Find purchase links for Bound by Sunlight at www.kbalan.com/books/bound-by-sunlight

To join KB Alan's newsletter, visit www.kbalan.com/newsletter

ALSO BY KB ALAN

Perfect Fit Series (Erotic Romance)
Perfect Formation (Book 1)
Perfect Alignment (Book 2)
Perfect Stranger (Book 2.5)
Perfect Addition (Book 3)
Perfect Temptation (Book 4)

Fully Invested (Contemporary Romance)
(Part of the Wildlife Ridge World)
Coming Home (Book 1)
Breaking Free (Book 2)
Finding Forever (Book 3)

Wolf Appeal Series (Paranormal Romance)
Alpha Turned (Book 1)
Challenge Accepted (Book 2)
Going Deeper (Book 3)

Stand Alone
Bound by Sunlight (Erotic Romance)
Keeping Claire (Fantasy Romance)
Sweetest Seduction (Contemporary Romance)

www.kbalan.com

ABOUT THE AUTHOR

KB Alan lives the single life in Southern California. She acknowledges that she should probably turn off the computer and leave the house once in a while in order to find her own happily ever after, but for now she's content to delude herself with the theory that Mr. Right is bound to come knocking at her door through no real effort of her own. Please refrain from pointing out the many flaws in this system. Other comments, however, are happily received.

www.kbalan.com

To join KB's newsletter, visit www.kbalan.com/newsletter

facebook.com/kbalan
twitter.com/KB_Alan
instagram.com/authorkbalan
bookbub.com/authors/kb-alan

Printed in Great Britain
by Amazon